WHO IS JOHN SHAFT?

A black Bogart who says the revolution is a new way to chase the chicks ... the Mafia is a meatball ... and life is going to screw you if you don't screw it. John Shaft is a private eye. John Shaft is a black man made of muscle and ice.

Shaft has no prejudices.
He'll kill anyone – black or white.

Shaft is big. Shaft is black.

The cloistered daughter of Harlem's black crime-boss discovers the true nature of her father's work and runs off to be as bad as Dad. Sex, liquor, dope and a few other scenes – she is into them all when she disappears. Big Daddy wants Big Shaft to get his baby back.

Shaft goes to work. And The Mafia, the Black Militants, the NYPD, and City Hall go to work on

SHAFT

Shaft
Ernest Tidyman

Bloomsbury Film Classics
The Original Novel

Series editors: Maxim Jakubowski and Adrian Wootton

First published by Macmillan 1971

This paperback edition first published by
Bloomsbury Publishing Plc 1997

This edition published by Bloomsbury Publishing Plc
for Sight and Sound magazine 2000

Bloomsbury Publishing Plc, 38 Soho Square, London W1V 5DF

A CIP catalogue record is available from the British Library

ISBN 0 7475 5398 X

10 9 8 7 6 5 4 3 2 1

Typeset by Hewer Text Ltd, Edinburgh
Printed in Great Britain by Clays Limited, St Ives plc

For

Grace Johnson,
Diane Schereschewsky,
Nancy Ware

Without whom
SHAFT
would have been impossible.

And
Constance Bogen,
Ronald Hobbs,
Judith Oppenheimer Loth,
Charles Mandlestam,
Warren Picower,
Jack Robbens,
Sylva Romano,
Leo Rosen,
Helen Sears,
Billie Jean Tidyman

Without whom
I
would have been impossible.

Chapter One

SHAFT FELT warm, loose, in step as he turned east at Thirty-ninth Street for the truncated block between Seventh Avenue and Broadway. It had been a long walk from her place in the far West Twenties. Long and good. The city was still fresh that early. Even the exhaust fans of the coffee shops along the way were blowing fresh smells, bacon, egg and toasted-bagel smells, into the fact of the gray spring morning. He had been digging it all the way. Digging it, walking fast and thinking mostly about the girl. She was crazy. Freaky beautiful. Crazy. They went out to dinner and she was wearing a tangerine wig and a long purple coat that looked like a blanket on a Central Park plug pulling one of those creaky carriages. It was the mood she was in and he had become a part of it. He never got back to his apartment. She wanted a night like that. They had it and, then, about 7:30, she handed him a glass of cardboard-container orange juice and began pushing him out of the apartment. It was their night, but the maid's day.

'Please, John. Hurry.'

Sitting on the edge of the bed, tying his shoes.

'Hey, you think that cleaning lady gives a shit about your morals? All she has in her head is twelve a day and tokens.'

'Just hurry. Go.'

He hurried, he went. It gave him time to kill. There was no point in turning back toward the Village and his own place.

His clothes were fresh. He had hardly worn them except for dinner. The subway or a cab would have been too quick for the trip to Times Square. So he walked. A big, black man in a gray lightweight wool suit moving quickly through the morning. The light at Thirty-ninth and Broadway caught him. He paused for a moment at the corner. The garment-district trucks were beginning to roll into the area. Shaft watched them and glanced north toward Times Square.

Sitting in his office up there, staring out at it when he had first found the rooms and moved in a desk, a chair, a filing cabinet and a few hopes, he had looked for a point of view, an attitude in Times Square. He failed to find it. He decided it was a giant pinball machine. The biggest goddamn pinball machine in the world. In the early morning, like now, it lay there dull and dusty. All the parts were scattered around. But nothing was working. The dime went into the slot about six in the evening, turning on the juice. Then the whole thing caught fire. The bumpers, bangers and zingers lighted up, and channels and traps glittered, the shimmering steel balls flashed from point to point while the score was emblazoned across the top half of it with shrieking glare. If it had a mystique, he thought, that was it: a big irresistible pinball machine. Go steal some more money from your mama's purse; we'll hit four million this time and win a free game. That was its point of view, its attitude. He liked it. It suited his needs for a temporary place.

Shaft began to pick up its vibrations as he waited for the WALK sign to flash green permission for the crossing. All that up Broadway a few blocks had become a part of him and was waiting for him. He stepped off the curb and moved easily around the grill of a battered Dodge truck, rolling with the contained grace of a solid, muscular man who stays in balance, who can land running or at a halt, poised to run again.

'I love to watch you get out of bed and go to the bathroom

or the window or the kitchen,' she said against his shoulder, a hand flat across the slab of pectoral on the right side of his chest, holding him, stroking him. 'You uncoil like an animal coming out of a cave.' He blew cigarette smoke at the ceiling. She could not see him smile. It was much too dark. Her hand moved from his chest across the flat ripple of muscles sheathing his stomach. It must have been 5 A.M., but it didn't matter. He could always sleep, he could always die. But he couldn't always do this. Not with someone like her.

The thought of her clung to him like her cologne. Shaft glanced up at the gleaming triangle of the Allied Chemical tower at Forty-second Street, then back at the driver of the cab inching toward him across the tattered white lines of the crosswalk. The driver's milky blue eyes were clouded. Maybe with fatigue from a night of cruising. Maybe with hate from a life of hacking. Honky Sonofabitch. Shaft stared him down. The cab stopped inching. One of these days, he would go over to Lexington to Uncle Sam's umbrella shop and order a bamboo-looking walking stick of Swedish steel to enforce a system of forfeits and penalties for cabs. Too close to the knees, one headlight. Too close to the back, a rear window. Slight physical contact, two headlights and the windshield, and if the driver got out of the cab . . . The worst they would bust him for was malicious mischief.

He skipped up onto the curb at Thirty-ninth Street, moving north. The coat, suit and fabric-laden trucks would turn these streets between Seventh and Sixth Avenues into a steel trap in the next fifteen to twenty minutes. He glanced at the steel-cased Rolex, face down on the underside of his left wrist. Eight-seven. Too early for anything. She had made him get up, nagged him through the quick shower. The parting kiss had been perfunctory and the push of her hand firm as he went through the door. He had a good memory

3

but the hardest thing in the world to remember seemed to be that he should stay away from there on Tuesday nights. For a girl with her body and her inclinations, her easiest thing seemed to be to make him forget that the maid came every Wednesday.

Vibrations. He felt again the slight signal of mood, the nuance of the atmosphere, that had brushed against him a block away. Shaft's bland face, an oval mask of black-brown skin about the color of a French-roast coffee bean, fell into the lines of a slight frown and he slackened the strong, march-time stride. What the hell was it? He walked his eyes up and down Broadway. Nothing. Nobody. There were three colored guys he knew standing in front of the Drago shoe repair shop just past Forty-first Street, wearing green cotton smocks and drinking coffee from containers from Whelan's on the corner or maybe from Schrafft's up past Forty-third. They knew him but they had not spotted him coming. There was no one around him on the street, just a few Puerto Rican kids getting to the garment racks they would be pushing through the streets all day. Shaft did not bother to be subtle. He turned to look behind him, down Broadway as it angled toward the crossing with Sixth Avenue (who called it the Avenue of the Americans outside *The New York Times*?) at Thirty-fourth Street. Nothing. Nobody. The cars and trucks were nondescript, one Fleetwood limousine among them hurrying someplace to pick up its passenger. The chauffeur was a chauffeur. The rear seat was empty. But Shaft still had the feeling. There was something; he had felt it before. He turned quickly into Fortieth Street and one of the curbside telephone booths.

'Nine-six-seven-five,' the operator answered.

'Good morning, Mildred. Shaft. Any calls?'

'Say, where've you been all night?'

'Mildred . . .'

'Somebody's been trying to get you all night,' she rattled on. 'I told them you were apparently unavailable.'

'Who?'

'They didn't say. They wouldn't say. You know I always try to get a name or a number.'

'I know you do. Man or woman?'

'Man. Men. Two of them, I think.'

'Any message?'

'They said as soon as you called you should leave a number where you could be reached. It was important.'

Shaft let the Cardex file of cases roll through his mind. Three divorces. A couple of pilferage things. One guy thought his partner was going to burn their warehouse. A couple of insurance claims in Harlem; the adjuster was afraid to go up there and handle them himself. Nothing important. Nothing anybody would want him for bad enough to stay up all night trying.

'They didn't leave a number?'

'Huh-uh. Sorry.'

'That's all right. Look, Mildred, if they call again, you still haven't heard from me. All right?'

'I got it.'

'Thanks. Talk to you later.'

'Oh, Mr. Shaft . . .'

'Yes.'

'What does it cost to get the goods on somebody for a divorce?'

'I don't know. Depends on who it is. How much time it takes. What kind of a case the lawyer wants, just testimony or the whole works with photographs and all that. Why? Who's it for?'

'Me. I think Emil is fooling around and you're the only private detective I know.'

5

Shaft looked east up Fortieth Street and saw the sun reaching down over the shoulders of the big buildings, paving the street with a moment of gold. He smiled.

'How old is Emil?'

'Sixty-three. But he's got ideas.'

'He still can't move very fast, Mildred. I'll give you a discount. Talk to you later.'

'I'll tell him what you said.'

She clicked off before he had a chance to protest. Poor Emil. Spending his last few years trying to leer up a miniskirt, worried about being followed by a private detective. At a discount. Poor John Shaft, trying to get to his office after being pushed off an overworked mattress, wondering who had spent the night looking for him. He was glad he had not taken her to his apartment. The number wasn't that difficult to get. And he had needed the night, wasting all the tension upon her and with her. She thought he was an animal. Let her think it. He was an animal. They were all animals together, only some of them had never rubbed raw the fat flesh of pretension. Let her think it. Let her need it. He walked.

The men looked up when he went by the Drago window, looked up and nodded in the rhythm of their bristle brushes and snapping shine cloths. They nodded but they did not smile. So they knew something. He would have to go back and find out what it was. Shaft walked to the corner of Forty-second Street, slipped the second copy of the *Times* from the stack at the blind vendor's kiosk, turned into the door of Whelan's.

'Container of black. No sugar.'

'Black. No sugar.'

She smiled at him. The constancy of glazed doughnuts had shot hell out of her smile. Apparently they had not gotten to her circulatory system yet. She could still smile over a coffee counter at eight-fifteen in the morning.

'Thank you. Please pay the cashier.'

Eight years ago, ten years ago, he would have been waiting out on the corner when she came out with the bag full of nickels and dimes. Eight years ago, ten years ago, maybe he would have grabbed the purse and run. Down Forty-second Street through the crowds, into the park behind the library, out into Fortieth Street and into Fifth Avenue scooping change into his pockets, throwing the purse into the shrubbery or the nearest trash basket. Keeping New York clean. Keeping himself alive. Would she have smiled at him then? Now she smiled at a tall black man in a gray suit and a blue shirt with a red silk tie. He was one of the new ones now. He left a quarter tip. He couldn't help himself even though only one of the old ones would do that – like the ones who were waiting for him with their shine cloths and brushes.

'John.'

'Hey, man.'

'Johnny.'

'Yeah.'

Each of them had a greeting as he went down the line to the last of the high chairs. As far as he could get from the garment-district hustlers in their polished plastic suits and opal pinky rings. He wasn't going out of the chute and into Times Square, into the place where he was expected to be, until he found out what the Drago crew knew and why they had not smiled. They were nodding. One of them would come tell him in a minute or so.

'Thank *you*, sir. You have a good day now.'

Somebody tipped a quarter. Somebody else couldn't help himself, looking down on those heads of men forty, fifty, sixty, twice the age and more of the men on the high perches. It was a very simple surgical process. You cut out the heart and took off the balls and put in two cans of Griffin or

Kiwi, one black, one brown, and you had a shine boy of forty, fifty, sixty.

'Watch the socks, Sam.'

Sam, why don't you cut off both his feet at the ankles, just for the hell of it? Then he won't need socks, will he? Sam, do you hear? Shaft punched the fold of the *Times* into a rigid rectangle that would stand against his knee while he pried the top off the coffee container and dropped it into the brown paper bag. He spilled a little coffee on his right pants leg, the drippings from the cap. It wouldn't stain. The suit was dark and it was the sugar and milk that stained. He began going over each headline before he started reading any of the articles. He learned long ago that *Times* readers had to do this. Otherwise, you lost whole events, world-shaking crises, in the typographical ants' nest through which they all had to crawl each morning. He was not familiar with many newspapers and he wondered if the *Times* was the only one that could hide a major event on its front page.

'Two of them,' the voice floated up to him.

He did not look from the paper to the thin, gray-haired man beginning to scrub an initial coat of black dye into his shoes. Shaft stared blankly at the page.

'Want to know where they might find a man who's so hard to find. Fast. Told to find him fast. Mmm, hmmm, mmm.'

The man began to hum when one of the customers returned from the cashier's desk after paying for the shine and dropped a dime into the old man's hand. He stood with the hand outstretched, the dime standing in lonely relief against the polish stains and calluses, a grain of sand on a sea of wrinkles, as the green suit hurried toward the door.

'Thank *you*, sir.'

The others broke up. Over the half-shined, almost-buffed

shoes down the line, they made the point of scorn for the cheap-ass Charlie.

'Some of these days,' one said, 'he gonna give you fifteen cents and make your whole day.'

The dime went into the flapfold of a pocket on the green, dye-spotted smock.

'I hope a building fall on that motherfucker. *That* gonna make my day.'

He played the scene and turned back to Shaft's plain-toed oxfords.

'Did they know me?'

'Sound like it.'

'Law?'

'Huh-uh.'

'Who?'

'Uptown.'

Uptown? Uptown, to this man, was north of 110th Street and the perimeter of Central Park. Uptown was Harlem and the shadow civilization sealed off by the great wall of fear. Shaft flipped the paper open to the editorial page with big, strong and meaty hands, broad across the pink palms, heavily veined on the back. Across the right hand was a twin track of saddle-stitch scar. It was a precise match and continuation of the inch-and-a-half track moving down his forehead toward his eyes. A few people noticed that the hand and head tracks connected. Women did. In bed. In the good afternoon light when they were appraising what they had discovered. He would raise his hand to his mouth with a cigarette and they could see the tracks connect. If he knew them well enough, he might explain how the bicycle chain had come whipping out of the vortex of a street fight and his hand had gone instinctively to his eyes. If the hand had not moved so swiftly, well, perhaps his eyes would not be there to search her own, to move across

9

her body and compare the color of her breast aureoles with the color of his fingers upon them. Where had it happened? they might ask. Uptown, he said. It happened uptown. I was trying to kill this cat and he didn't think I should do that. I was trying to kill myself and he was helping me.

Shaft looked at a Reston column and said softly, 'Do I know them?'

'You should.'

Shaft could not press the old man. He had to let him play his own part of the communications conspiracy that existed between them. It was a way of giving value to the information – and to the man. But it was slow. A circuitous grinding of the kernels of inference and implication into a fact on which he might act. That somebody was after him was secondary. They were coming, one way or another. It was why that counted. And something about that motivation had stiffened the context of his relationship with these men in the shine parlor. It was an indirect threat, but still a threat.

'Mob?'

'Not their kind.' The old man nodded toward the Italian manager and head shoemaker at the rear of the shop.

'Uptown.' Shaft was saying it to himself.

'Uptown,' the old man echoed, finishing the glittering shine, tapping the soles of Shaft's shoes in the traditional signal.

Shaft climbed down with long-legged fluidity, paid the cashier thirty-five cents for the shine, tipped the old man a quarter and handed him the *Times*. He would find the ten-dollar bill spread out across James Reston's remarks about Nixon when he took the paper into the toilet or some other place of momentary privacy. Shaft would take the ten dollars and maybe the price of the shine back from whoever had made it necessary. One way or the other. It was like that.

He took the wide, deep, dark glasses from the breast pocket

of his jacket and slipped them over his eyes as he walked toward
the thick glass door, stopped there a moment to resettle the gray
straw hat on the center of his forehead. His hand was on the
glass, already beginning to push as the plain green Plymouth
pulled up tight against the curb and the driver turned a flat,
dull face toward the shop. Shaft couldn't connect the name.
But he knew the face. A 17th Precinct face. Even behind the
reflecting glass of the shades they both wore, Shaft felt their
eyes lock for a moment and saw the face nod to him. He was
supposed to walk over to the green Plymouth, while everybody
in the Drago shine line was digging it, and talk with the Man.
Fuck him and anybody else who tried that shit. Shaft pushed
the door, stepped out on the sidewalk and turned north in a
quick spin. Ready to run. First it was strangers in the night,
now it was police. What the hell was going on . . . that he
had to know about before he talked with any of them? He
was not going in blind.

'Johnny?' Shaft let the call from the car bounce off his back.
He picked up the speed of his stride. Left. He'd fall into the
morning traffic pushing down Broadway now, let the bastards
blow their horns, let the 17th Precinct watch him through the
rear-view mirror. There were three honeycomb buildings on
Forty-second between Seventh and Eighth that he could get
in and out of fast, ducking a tail. He could get someplace
and on the telephone to find out why he was so suddenly in
demand.

They were beside him just as he started to cut around the
subway entrance at Forty-second and across Broadway. Two
more faces from the 17th. They had set him up for this.
Whatever they wanted, they were working like hell to get
it. They even sent a whole live lieutenant of detectives after
it. He could go right through them and run. Or he could stop
and deal. He stopped.

'Shaft,' said Anderozzi. Tense, tight, waiting for Shaft's play.

'Lieutenant. You're out early.'

'It's late. Depends on when you start.'

'Okay, Lieutenant, you're out late.'

Anderozzi untensed; Shaft wasn't going to run. The other face beside the lieutenant's was blank, silent. Waiting. The eyes were over his shoulder. Shaft figured the other was coming up behind him. Boxed. The morning swarms were disengorging themselves from the entrails of the subway, flowing around them, rubbing against them. A static little island in the flood.

'I want you to come back to the car and talk with me for a minute or so.'

Anderozzi delivered the line straight. There was no threat, no demand. It was just what he wanted at that moment. Shaft could accept, refuse or screw up the conversation. He decided to make it as difficult as possible; he was very angry at being boxed.

'Why?'

'I'll tell you when we talk.'

'Now.'

'In the car.'

'Now.'

'No.'

'Then fuck it. And all the rest of this ball-breaking bullshit.'

If they were going to bust him, they were going to have to do it right here on the corner. He wasn't going back past the Drago window in the quiet company of three white cops. They had given it the structure of a confrontation, not he. The big one next to the lieutenant was settling back on his heels to throw one. Good. He'd never know what hit him.

'Take him first, Johnny,' the lieutenant said with a nod to the plainclothesman. 'I'm too old for you.'

'I was thinking of the one behind me.'

The lieutenant smiled, but not with teeth.

'He's not there. He's still in the car.'

'I figure I got just enough time to find out.'

'Let's talk, Shaft.' The lieutenant had a thin, gray face and black hooded eyes. He was as tall as Shaft, just under six feet, but much leaner, and the way he stood made Shaft think of sharp objects. The lieutenant looked like a linoleum knife, ready to cut. The big beak of a nose made it complete.

'We're talking.'

'Not here.'

'Look, Lieutenant. You want to tell me something, tell me. You want to ask me something, ask me. You want to talk with me, call me at my office and we'll make an appointment and we'll talk. We'll talk all night if you want. But not you, not him . . . and he better know I'm going to break it off him and make him eat it . . . and not the guy behind me. None of you is going to push me in that car back there unless I know why we're going, where we're going and how long we're going and somebody else, somebody on my side maybe, knows that I'm going.'

'Take it easy, John.'

'Take it easy, my ass! I'm taking it the way it's being fed to me right now and I'm giving it right back to you.'

'Look, Lieutenant,' the cop started to say.

'Shut up.' He was a big piece of cheese. Anderozzi was the knife. 'Go back to the car. Take stupid there with you.'

The detective did as he was told. Shaft could feel the threat behind him melt away.

'All right, John. We'll talk here.' The lieutenant did not look around or concern himself about who might overhear. He was looking one way, Shaft was looking the other. Between them, they probably knew every face in the city, black or white, that

13

should not be a party to the conversation. 'All right. They've been looking for you all night. Uptown. Downtown. Even in the Village. How the hell you got all the way up here without running into them, I don't know.'

'I walked.'

'That's probably it. Only you and about eight other crazy bastards in this city walk anywhere.'

'Sometimes I run.'

'So do I. Right now I got instructions to run like hell until I find out if they want you for something I should know about.'

The lieutenant waited.

'Go ahead.'

'I want it straight, John. I have to know what's going on.'

'What do you *think's* going on?'

Lieutenant Victor Anderozzi, head of a special investigative detail assigned to the 17th Precinct in the name of (and under the sole order of) the Commissioner of Police, sighed. He took Shaft's arm and started to walk with him around the corner of the drugstore, down Forty-second Street toward Sixth Avenue. Two men walking arm in arm as scholars might walk through the Sorbonne.

'You know, John, thirty years ago I used to go up-state fishing with my old man. I loved fishing. Sitting in a little leaky boat. The old man let me bail it with a can. Catching bluegills, sunfish, perch. Catfish once in a while. I used to love fishing. Now I hate it. I can't stand the thought of it. I think that for the last twenty-three years I've been doing nothing but fishing inside people. I've come up with the goddamnedest collection of tin cans, old tires and other pieces of garbage.'

Two fags walked by, heading toward the men's rooms in the twenty-four-hour movie grind houses between Seventh and Eighth. They smiled at the way Anderozzi was holding Shaft's arm. They stopped smiling when Anderozzi glanced at them with the knife of his gray face.

'I hate it. But here I am again because somebody says I have got to go fishing, trying to find out what's beginning to bite at the bottom of a very dark lake.'

'Sometimes you get poetic, Vic.'

They stopped at the Wurlitzer window and looked at the black and brown pianos for ten dollars down and two lifetimes of payments.

'Don't get cocky. I talk to my kids just like this before I beat up on them.'

'I'm not one of your kids. And you're fishing.'

'I'm fishing.'

'Would you believe me if I said I didn't have the vaguest goddamned idea of what's going on except that somebody has come down from Harlem and spent the whole night looking for me. Would you believe that's all I know?'

'I guess I would.'

'Then that's what I'm telling you. I'm also asking. What the hell *is* this?'

'Let's go over to that nut joint on the other side and get some hot cashews. I love the things. They give me heartburn, but I can't stop.'

They were across Sixth, turning toward the Nuts to You shop when Shaft asked, 'Are you walking me away from Times Square?'

The lieutenant did not reply. He bought Shaft a quarter pound of natural pistachios, got his own cashews, then walked him across the street to Bryant Park, where the winos sleep and the fags prowl behind the backs of the almost complete works of civilization in the marble library.

There was an empty bench that early in the day.

'Something has happened, the way I get it, that has turned on

15

the gas under the kettle up there.' He was popping hot cashews into his mouth, chewing, swallowing and talking all at once. 'We don't know what. But something. Black cops, white cops, cops up there and down here. They have been hearing things. All kinds of things about the Mob, the Muslims, the old bunch, the militants. Christ, everybody. You never saw so many cops who were hearing things.' He paused for two cashews, then a third. 'And you never saw so many *scared* cops.'

'What do they hear?'

'That something has happened to cut it all up and to set it all off. That the whole goddamned thing is going to turn into the biggest war, criminal, racial or any name you want to give it, that the city has ever seen. That in the next week or so there is going to be blood on every street in the city. That is what they hear.'

'Oo-ee,' Shaft whistled. 'But why?'

'I don't know. Goddamnit, I don't know. But you? You're the one who should. Some people from up there are suddenly looking for you so hard that they spread the word all over town, where even my twelve-year-old daughter could pick it up and report home with it. I want to know why. I have been told very definitely that I must know why immediately.'

Shaft thought about it. War? There was no faction in Harlem ready for war. Not now. Not yet. Some of them might want it, lust for it with all the encapsuled violence it was possible to pack into a man. They exploded in sorties and skirmishes. They released their fury in warnings and threats. But they did not come to the point, not yet, when it was open, bloody war. On anything. Or anybody.

'It is probably going to come some day,' Shaft said.

'Don't test me. There is a revolution going on in this city and every other city. I know it, even if I am just a cop. Or maybe because I'm Anderozzi and not somebody else. That's

16

one thing, that revolution. This is another. This is what has been fermenting for the last forty-eight hours, not for a century. This is what may be happening tonight, not in the next week, the next month, the next year. This is what they are going to be carrying into the emergency rooms in wicker baskets about three o'clock tomorrow morning. You want me to have a philosophy? I do. My philosophy is to see that it doesn't happen now, whatever it is.'

Shaft flicked pistachio shells into the bushes and looked around the park. Anderozzi was right. For Anderozzi. Everybody was right for himself. Truth is subjective. It is also negotiable.

'What do you want from me?'

'If you don't know anything now, I'll settle for a call – ' Anderozzi pushed back the sleeve of his brown sports jacket to his watch, a thin gold circle with a gold mesh band – 'in about twelve hours. That's nine tonight when I'll hear from you.'

'One thing.'

'Why not?'

'The guy behind me. He isn't there, or anywhere.'

'You'll be able to tell. Talk to you later.'

'Talk to you.'

Shaft left the lean, gray man feeding nuts to a lean, gray squirrel. He cut across Forty-second Street at the light and began moving up the east side of Sixth Avenue, catching the reflections in the windows of the stores, the tobacco shop and the watchmaker. There was nothing behind him. Just the nine-o'clock crush of leaking paper bags attached to people. He tuned them out. They were not part of his morning. He had been hunted, threatened, boxed and lectured through a sixty-minute kaleidoscope in which he was the dominant crystal. Yet he had been almost entirely without control over the changing patterns or the infusion of light. There had been better mornings. He felt as if he were being asked to walk across an empty stage, under the blinding beam of an arc light, while an auditorium of hostile strangers judged a performance in which he had been given no rehearsal. Goddamn the whole bunch of them. What was he supposed to do? A tap dance on the head of a pin while they threw molotovs at him?

Shaft moved across Sixth at Forty-third and walked up to an electronics gadget and equipment shop. Fisher, Bogen, Garrard. Three choices. He had three choices. He could hole up in the Village until he found out why. He could make the rounds, make the connections until they ran across each other and maybe it was cool and maybe it wasn't. He could go after them, run them down and make them pay for the morning. He liked that idea, his anger rising to meet it, a gut twist of warmth. He opened the gate of it just a little wider, caught it and shaped it into the small ball of energy. Fuel. He would burn just a little at a time; it was all he needed. Just enough to get across the message that when you wanted John Shaft, you sought his attention politely in the proper manner, with the respect he merited as a man. You didn't make trouble for him. You didn't come clumsy, tough and evil into his place and try to make it yours, to run it your way. You knew what you were doing every minute or he was going to show you. John Shaft was going to teach you some manners.

He chose Forty-sixth Street and turned west. A little more slowly now. Every face that passed him on the street became a deposit of his memory bank. The cars pushing east against the first morning traffic jam went through his search. One of the public entrances to his building was halfway down the block. The other was around the corner, north, fronting on Times Square. He knew of three others. One out back, the fire exit. One through the shoe shop on the corner. And this one, through the little store that sold the sex books over the counter and off the racks, the packets of photographs under the counter and out of the pocket. The Forty-sixth Street branch library of the Times Square voyeur.

The operator of the store looked up from the register and the small counter, nodded and said nothing. Shaft had been that route before. The men at the racks flicked through the pages, studied the introductions, never looked up. It was the one place in the world where nobody looked up into the eyes of anyone else. No faces, no eyes. Only into the books and the fantasies.

Shaft slipped down one of the tight aisles to the rear and the door marked 'No Entrance, Employees Only.' He pulled it open and stepped into a long, narrow corridor, moving quickly past the open doors of a small office, a storeroom, a toilet, twenty feet down the dark hallway to the door at the end. He turned the latch of the triple-bolt lock, eased it open a crack and looked into the building's stairwell hallway. Empty.

He ducked into a crouch to move out. The door in the stairwell leading into the building lobby was half glass, half steel. He started to go for the stairs, then turned to the lobby door, holding himself flat against the gray, dusty wall to peek out. The elevator starter was ushering the morning arrivals into the cars. Some office girls were stopping at the magazine-cigar stand for cigarettes and chewing gum. And there, there was one of them. The sonofabitch. Shaft could hardly believe it. Did they still make them that way?

The tall, angularly thin Negro wore a double-breasted brown suit two sizes too large. Large enough to get a .38 in the belt without a bulge. Or maybe something smaller or bigger. Standing in front of the book rack, probably worrying the counterman about whether some of his cheap volumes were going to be lifted. Probably worrying everybody who came

19

through the rundown, unpolished lobby en route to the offices of second-rate lawyers, small show-business types, a couple of novelty merchandise jobbers and John Shaft Investigations. Standing with one eye on the book rack, the other on the lobby. Dumb John Shaft would come through the lobby, get on the elevator, and this one would step quickly after him. A very simple box. The one upstairs would help him tie the ribbon on it when they got up there. The stupid sonofabitch.

Shaft eased open the door, stepped into the lobby and paused. It was about ten steps to the man's back. Shaft waited for the elevator starter to pack in another load and turn toward the entrances. All he needed was 'Good morning, Mr. Shaft.' That's all. The starter saw the doors closed and turned. Now Shaft moved. Now she could have called him animal and known what it meant. Ten steps? He took it in four swift strides. As the ball of his left foot touched on the last of them, his right hand came up, palm down, fingers welded together and straight out like a spear. He drove it exactly eight inches, thrusting into the relaxed flesh of the slender sentinel, just at the kidney, slightly behind and below the rib cage. Flesh, muscle, tissue tore beneath the thrust.

'Aiyee,' the man gasped. Then the pain took him out and he began to fold like a marionette whose strings have been slashed. Shaft threw an arm around his waist, one hand finding the outline of the gun beneath the coat, and held him up.

Marty at the cigar counter kept handing chewing gum to stenos.

'Hello, Jimmy,' Shaft said to the elevator starter.

'Good morning, Mr. Sh . . . say, what happened to . . .?'

'Friend of mine. Has fainting spells. Let me get him up to the office for a drink of water.' Pour water into this one and it would come out blood. For a long time.

'Sure thing, Mr. Shaft. Just a minute, folks. Man sick here. Take this car. Go ahead.'

Shaft pushed the button for the third floor, tore the gun out of the sagging waistband and stuck it into his right rear pocket. Forty-five revolver. Colt's old army model. It was insane. What did they think this was, 1932? Insane.

He dragged the crumpled rag doll out of the car at the third floor and straight down the hallway to his own office door. Some typewriters were already going behind the others. There would be people off the next car in a few seconds. He propped his wheezing burden against the wall directly opposite the entrance to his office, knocked sharply and stepped aside.

'Hey, what the hell . . .?' said the head that poked out of the door and stared in a moment of surprise. A moment in which the guillotine of Shaft's arm descended. It took the head just behind the left ear. He had them both inside before the sick *thwack* had echoed around the corner and down the hall to the nowhere of silence.

Shaft pushed a finger at the collection on the top of his desk blotter. They had to be out of their minds. Or to want him so badly that recklessness of this sort was not a consideration. The black cannon of a .45 gleaming with the oil of attention and care, as big as a giant turkey leg next to the nickel-plated .38 from the pocket of the other one. Nobody carried heat like that into Times Square, nobody but a maniac looking for a President to kill. With a couple of long-blade knives and a nasty little gadget that the burlier of the two, the one who had been in his office, probably made himself. A piece of industrial belt or strap, studded with brass screw heads, the two ends of the strap forming a loop where they attached to a three-inch length of lead, about an inch in circumference. The loop went over the fingers and around the knuckles while the hand closed on the lead cylinder. A short, hard blow with that would tear a man's jaw off. It could kill and cripple. It might have killed and crippled him if they had not been so clumsy and stupid.

Shaft looked at them, propped against the wall beside the desk. The skinny one was wheezing and groaning with the agony of his torn kidney, the other silent and unconscious while a small trickle of blood wandered down the side of his chin like a country road on a black topographical map. Shaft's own stomach muscles were clutched in the spasms of tension, anger, and so much adrenalin was pouring through his system that he felt the soaring capacity to do anything anywhere, to fling open the window and run up the side of the building to the twentieth floor before gravity noticed he was gone. But he gave no sign of it. His hand was completely steady as he shook a Kent from one of the packages he had scooped out of their pockets along with the armament, the wads of ten-dollar bills both had been carrying, keys and a miscellany of matches, coins. No wallets, no identification, no names.

The match flared and he drew deeply and swallowed the smoke, letting it trail out his nose. Waiting, calming down, he began flipping through the mail that had been pushed through the slot in the door. A couple of ads for office services. A letter from the Pinkertons asking if he could make himself available again for assignment as night porter at Bergdorf-Goodman to deal with the pilferage problem. A couple of weeks work as an anonymous black face. The rate was good but it screwed up his social life. A letter from Damrosch, Pinott & Sullivan, Attorneys at Law, including a check for $756.22 for services rendered to a client who was now free to remarry and provide more employment for lawyers and private detectives, if not to mention motel clerks. Shaft put the check in his wallet, making a mental note to send it on to his accountant, Marvin Green. An almost indecipherable postcard from somebody in Athens. Who the hell did he know making the scene in Athens? The name was either Josie, Josiah, Josip or Josh and none of them meant anything. He threw it in the square green metal wastebasket. Nothing much. Nothing to worry about.

He pulled over the desk calendar. Nothing there, either. It was, as he recalled, to be a day to clean up odds and ends, maybe go looking for some new furniture for the office. It depressed him, in its simple, uniform plainness. Anybody who came into the office probably thought of used furniture first and Shaft second. It needed a taste of dignity, class. He was going to run over to the Itkin showroom and see a guy who could deal a discount. Later. He could do it later. It would not make that much difference. The immediate and sole problem he had was there on the floor beside the desk. Half of it was moving slightly, groaning and coming back to consciousness.

Shaft reached for the .45, hefted it in his hand and flipped open the cylinder with a thumb-flick of the catch and a shake of his wrist. All six chambers loaded. The stupid bastard didn't even know enough to keep the firing pin on an empty chamber. Drop the piece one day, it lands on the hammer and accidentally blows your ass off. It infuriated him anew that the estimate of his presence, if not his importance, should be so lightly made that clowns like this would be sent to seek him out. He glanced out the window. The day was clearing up. It would be breezy, bright and sunny, he thought, pulling back the hammer on the .45.

The big one began blinking. Maybe the noise of the steel clicking into place on the big gun in Shaft's hand had cut through the murk of his confusion. Shaft watched the man's eyes roll, shift left and right and come into focus. Shaft fixed them by raising the gaping muzzle of the pistol and pointing it directly at the flat, flaring nose between those eyes. They locked on the barrel, then lifted to Shaft's own. There was no fear there, but hatred so raw and violent that Shaft wondered what his own face might be reflecting.

'What do you want?' Shaft demanded.

The other one just looked at him, raising the back of his left hand slowly to wipe away the blood on his chin, then glancing down at it. Finally he said, 'Man I'm gonna kill your ass.'

Shaft pushed his chair back with his left hand, kept himself in a low leaning crouch and held the gun straight out and steady. His finger on the trigger was less than a hair, less than a feather. But it was there and the man on the floor could see it. Shaft reached over with his left hand to the skinny one, crumpling the grotesquely wide lapels of the double-breasted brown suit in his fist. He moved back, raising the gangling form with him, staying in the crouch, keeping the gun steady and aimed. Then he spun and whipped.

Every taut muscle of Shaft's body went into the twist and turn, the wrench of his arm and the lash of his wrist. The limp, bent form in brown danced, skated and angled crazily through the open space between the desk and the window. The glass exploded against the head and shoulders of the projectile. It crashed and clattered and tinkled as the body went hurtling through and out into the bright, breezy, sunny spring day.

He had not moved the gun more than six or eight inches. The eyes locked on it began to fill and bulge with fear as the last shards of glass sprinkled the pavement and screams of shock and horror rose from the sidewalk. Tires chewed noisily into the asphalt, car and truck horns exchanged insults with the buses, and the wind ruffled the papers on Shaft's desk. His voice sounded almost casual, cool, but the tone of it cut through the wave of noise as a dark dorsal fin cuts the night sea.

'Going to kill my ass, huh?' The man on the floor was turning to two hundred pounds of chocolate pudding in a blue suit. Rivulets of perspiration ran down his face, dropped onto a yellow tie. 'Well, you got two minutes. Maybe. Two minutes before they come up here and ask me why I threw that sonofabitch out the window. Then the man is going to ask me why I shot you right through the head. You hear? Right through the fucking head like you was the worst kind of dog in the world. You hear?'

The first siren was keening toward Times Square.

'You hear that? That's the meat rack from the morgue coming to take you home. So now you answer me. You answer me straight. And maybe you got two minutes, maybe a minute and a half. And maybe I'll listen.'

The man began to stammer and blubber.

'Knocks said we was to get you and bring you. Knocks said . . . Knocks said you was to come up and talk with him. Knocks said he didn't care what, you was to . . .'

Shaft gazed at the man and listened, but his mind was moving off. A vision of Knocks Persons began filtering through it, a vision of gargantuan proportions, of glittering automobiles, flashing diamonds. Numbers runners, pushers, hustlers, the smoky, seedy bars of side-street Harlem – they moved through the vision, too, becoming a part of the conglomerate Knocks Persons. The man on the floor had nothing more to tell him. This was just an errand boy with a screw-studded, lead-weighted fist and chrome-glittering .38 to help him tie up the packages. Shaft was insulted. Send a boy to fetch a boy. He heard a commotion developing in the corridor outside the offices and he considered pulling the trigger. Squeeze it off right into the middle of the furrows of fright that covered the wet, ugly face. But he would never get the wall clean and he hated the sinus-corroding fumes of fresh paint. And why bother? Knocks Persons would get the message from the fallen pigeon being scraped off the pavement below.

Chapter Two

THE DAY was shot. It went out the window with that fool. It went over to the new precinct offices on East Fifty-first Street. The Homicide people got a piece of it. So did the smart-ass young assistant district attorney. Questions, answers. Statements. How did he cover the lobby scene? The first one put the arm on him there, he said, was taking him up to the office to finish the job.

'What did he say to you?'

'Which one?'

'The first one. We'll have his name in a couple of minutes.'

'He said he was going to blow my mother-fucking brains out.'

'It was definitely a threat on your life?'

'It wasn't an invitation to go roller skating.'

'Mr. Shaft, I am trying to establish the reason why a man died this morning.'

'Mr. Shapiro, I am only trying to tell you why he was the one who died . . . and I wasn't.'

Shaft gambled. He bet the elevator starter and the cigar-stand proprietor would not want to remember how it had happened. The two black men? What two black men? Got no trouble with coloreds around here, buddy; why don't you guys chase all the winos and queers out of Times Square? Get the pigeons while you're at it. Shaft bet the cops wouldn't care that much. A

27

body in Times Square was as easy to ignore as a baboon in a ballroom. But a dead spade is a dead spade. Who in blue really gave a shit? Shaft gambled. The newspaper and television reporters tried to get a piece of the day. They failed. No pictures. Shaft's occupation made it necessary for him to remain as anonymous as possible, he said. He wanted to cooperate, of course. But they understood. Go take a picture of Times Square. Go interview a cop.

Lieutenant Anderozzi rescued him from the energy-sucking remainder of it. He turned up late in the morning, noted that the two men who had accosted Shaft were thoroughly documented acquaintances of the law as thieves, takers and sellers of narcotics, carriers of dangerous weapons, dealers in mayhem and malevolence and had been a considerable drain on the time and tax dollars of the city. If anything, he suggested, they should be billed for repairs to Shaft's window.

'I think it will wash,' Anderozzi said, looking up from the report he had been reading to the wing-tip oxfords hooked on the corner of his desk. 'We told the papers they were probably looking for narcotics in a dentist's office in the building. I hope there *is* a dentist in the building.'

Shaft raised his chin from his chest. He had almost gone to sleep in the butt-cupping grip of the molded steel chair.

'Don't know. May be. Place has got everything else, including a couple of chicks on the tenth floor operating a tour service that will take you around the world for fifty dollars a trip.'

'That's nice. It gives you something to do with your lunch hours. Listen, I think this will wash but you're technically charged with homicide. We will all have to go down to the district attorney's office and do a routine for them about what a couple of bad bastards these guys were.'

'Black bastards.'

'Bad bastards. Don't be paranoid.'

'You pretty fancy.'

'I used to take night classes.'

The door to the small office opened and a squarely built plainclothesman walked in carrying a slip of paper, sleeves rolled up over beefy forearms, pants bagging and sagging under the weight of the pistol in the waistband holster, handcuffs dangling from the belt, a blackjack and report journal crammed into back pockets. He nodded at Shaft. Shaft nodded back.

'This is the number.' He handed the slip to Anderozzi, turned to leave as the lieutenant got his long legs down off the desk and came to something like attention.

'Thanks. Tony?'

'Yessir?'

'Reporters and TV people all gone?'

'About ten minutes ago.'

'Thanks.'

Anderozzi got a ballpoint out of the desk drawer and copied the number onto a scratch pad. He handed the slip to Shaft.

'Knocks will answer. And only Knocks. It's going to surprise hell out of him to hear the lovely baritone of John Shaft coming out of it.'

'Why? What is it?'

'A pay phone in his closet.' Anderozzi laughed lightly. 'It's the only one he uses to call his ex-wife. About once a week he goes into the closet and calls her. He listens to her complain about her apartment, the clothes she needs, the money she wants, the car she just wrecked, the people who are dumping on her. Like that until the operator breaks in and says, "Five cents more for five more minutes, please." It's a pay phone, right? Knocks tells her he hasn't got any change, that he'll call her back later, and hangs up. That's it for a week. The telephone just sits there waiting. And if it rings, he answers and explains it's a wrong number.'

Shaft laughed, too. Most of the tension of the day had drained out of him. But he was nowhere near the free, floating spirit he had felt coming up Seventh Avenue that morning. A little more human now, more in touch with himself, but still not right. He got out of the chair, stretched out on the floor and began doing pushups.

'How the hell did he get a pay phone in his closet?'

Anderozzi counted ten, eleven, twelve and wondered if he could still pass ten himself.

'Just asked the telephone company to stick it there. Guaranteed them the average take in dimes each month.'

'Who found it?'

'Internal Revenue. Tax people were throwing a bug on every wire in and out of his place last year and they came across this one. They crossed connections while they were hooking it up and an operator came on demanding that they deposit a dime.'

Shaft's amusement was making it almost impossible to continue. He squeezed out the twenty-eighth push-up and got up, dusting his hands off, palm against palm.

'Pretty clean floor. How'd they fix the operator?'

'Same way Persons does. Told her they didn't have any change and got the hell out of there.'

When they stopped laughing, Shaft asked, 'Tax people after Persons now?'

'Everybody's after him. We are, they are. For all I know, the CIA is.'

Shaft remembered a story about the old Mafioso, Frank Costello, who used to pick up his telephone each day to summon his chauffeur and deliver a general greeting to the assorted crackles and beeps on his line: 'Good morning, everybody.'

'I guess I'll split. Got to make a phone call.'

'Want to make it here?'

'No.'

'One thing, John.'

'Yes?'

'You know Persons?'

'I'm from Harlem, man, remember? Just because I live in the Village, wear a beret and walk a little funny, that don't mean . . .'

Anderozzi was serious. The detective leaned over the desk on his elbows, his hands on his face, pulling the flesh away from the eyes. He looked like a skinny Halloween mask, remotely connected to the cap gun dangling in a shoulder holster beneath his left arm-pit.

'No. Have you ever talked with him or met him?'

'Saw him a couple of times. That's all.'

'He's mean, John. Tough, ruthless, smart, cunning and mean.'

'I dig all that. We call it evil.'

'He's evil in any language. Seeing him and going up against him is a new ball game. Six or seven hours ago you killed one of his people. I don't know whether you had to or not. I don't give a damn. But Knocks Persons cares.'

'Come on, Vic, what is this shit? So he's a big-time racketeer in Harlem. So he *owns* Harlem. So what? He wants to take me out, let him try.'

'People have been saying that for thirty years.'

'What people?'

'You wouldn't know them. They're all dead.'

Shaft paused. They stared intently at each other for a moment.

'He knows I'm here, he knows that I won't go up there uncovered and he knows now that I won't play games in his own grown-up Disneyland. At least not his game. What's he going to do?'

'Anything he damn well pleases. He always has. That's one of the things that worries me about this.'

'I'll give you a ring.'

'I hope so.'

Shaft was almost out the door when the detective called to him, 'Hey, John.'

'Yes.'

'Is this right in the report? You're twenty-eight?'

'Yes. Why?'

'How'd you get so crazy so young?'

The air was soft and cooling against Shaft's face when he stepped out of the precinct and into Fifty-first Street, turned left toward Third Avenue. There was enough breeze to carry away the stink of the midday traffic snarl. He was looking for a telephone. The one hanging on the wall in the coffee shop on Third near Forty-sixth Street.

'Change a quarter, please.'

'What?'

The silly faggot jumped about three inches out of his bright blue raglan sweater and its powder-puff sleeves. What did he think it was, a stickup?

'Can you change a quarter, please?'

'Oh, certainly sir.' Black eyes glittered nervously, hopefully in a too pale, too soft face.

'Thanks.'

He felt like a contestant in the Miss America pageant. The creep was undressing him as he walked to the phone. Third Avenue: the meat rack. Go to the can anywhere in this neighborhood and they came out of the woodwork for you, chirping and tweeting. Shaft got the slip of paper from his jacket, dropped a dime in the slot and dialed. He looked up at the cashier. The eyes were still devouring him. Shaft smiled warmly, affectionately, knowingly at the cashier. The little cocksucker would probably whip his dum-dum right out of the socket about four o'clock tomorrow morning in a frenzy of frustration. Just thinking about the smile. Shaft winked at him as the phone rang for the fourth time and the receiver was lifted.

Knocks Persons just sat there. Massive, mountainous, a great brown mound of a man in a black suit completely filling the white leather chair that looked like a vertical bathtub on a chrome base with casters. Everything around him in the big open room was larger than life. The white walls rose thirty or thirty-five feet to the ceiling and disappeared into the mists of soft lighting. The long, wide glass desk at which he sat might have been a Macy's display window set horizontally on chromed sawhorses. Even the liquor bottles along the back of the thirty-foot ebony bar across the room were half-gallon bottles rather than fifths. All of it, from the fleecy carpeting that turned the floor into a snow-covered gridiron to the African prints hanging on the walls in silvery frames, was in varying shades of black and white.

Knocks Persons sat there staring without seeing any of it. He had been there for more than twenty-four hours. Occasionally one of the telephones on the long desk-shelf behind him would ring softly and demand he turn to deal with it. His answers were grunts or monosyllabic rumbles from the deep cavern of his chest. Then he would turn back to look out across the clear, glimmering top of the glass lake through which nothing swam except the polished, pointed toes of his classically simple shoes. Instead of the place and the comfortable prospects of it, he was seeing a private panorama that played only on the inside of his skull. A vision of life past and present, the life

33

he had lived and thought he understood. Where? Where? he asked with each new scene that moved into focus and drifted away. Where? He could not find the answer and, not finding it, he could not act. He could only sit and stare and wait. For the first time in his life, he was feeling pain. Deep, clear and immobilizing pain. And he was stunned. Where was the flaw? Where?

The phone rang and he almost turned to pick up one of the receivers behind him. It rang a second time and he looked toward the dressing-room closet door at the left of the desk. The door to a place where twenty black suits were hanging beside one hundred white shirts, next to forty pairs of elegantly simple black shoes, with thirty white silk ties, all waiting with a slightly antique pay telephone for Knocks Persons to need them. He got up from the desk at the start of the third ring and moved toward the closet, shaven head gleaming in the soft indirect light, folds of flesh around his bull neck amost hiding the collar of his shirt. A lumbering giant whose police records described him as a fraction over 6 feet 6 inches tall, weighing 290 pounds with distinct scars in at least eleven places on his massive body. For purposes of identification, as the records said.

On the fourth ring, his huge hand swallowed the receiver, put it to his ear. He leaned down to grumble 'Wrong number' when a voice said, 'This is John Shaft, you nigger sonafabitch, and I'm ready when you are.'

Shaft had two ideas after the talk with Persons. He was going to get loose and he was going to get laid.

'Goodbye, there,' the cashier sang to him.

Shaft leaned over the counter to whisper.

'You know where the boathouse is in Central Park?'

The fag nodded eagerly. Shaft looked at his watch.

'I'll be there about twelve-forty-five. No, make that one A.M.
sharp. Okay?'

'Do we have to meet in the park?'

'Well, if you don't want to . . .'

'Oh, all right.'

'*Ciao*.'

'*Ciao*.'

The muggers and that one deserved each other. He hoped
the little fart was a karate champion; he would last about ten
minutes longer that way. Until somebody stuffed his brown
belt in one ear and pulled it out the other. Knotted.

Cabs were crowding up Third Avenue with women shoppers,
some businessmen getting back from lunch too smashed to see.
He wanted a drink, too. A lemonade pitcher full of them.

Shaft leaned off the curb and flagged three cabs before
the driver of one would recognize his existence. Now that
cops were moonlighting as armed cab drivers, it was almost
possible for a black man to travel overland through New
York. If his wardrobe passed the meticulous inspection of
the cigar-stinking, unshaven ragbag behind the wheel. It was
such a waste of energy being black. Emotional and physical.

'McBurney YMCA, please. It's on West Twenty-third Street
just west of Seventh.'

'You wanna go down the Drive?'

'No, I wanna go down Park Avenue to Twenty-third Street
and turn right.'

'You're the boss.'

Shaft grunted. Persons had surprised him. Anderozzi said
Shaft's voice would shake Persons. He had expected violent
anger, equal to and possibly surpassing his own. It had not
been there. At least not on the surface. He read it as a tired
old man, a limping giant looking for a cave where he could
hide from the pygmies. Hide and bleed awhile. But thinking of

35

Persons that way was deadly dangerous. That wasn't Knocks Persons, not the legend nor the lumbering mammoth in the flesh. Persons had been shot, cut, smashed over the head, run down, slammed so deep into jail moles couldn't find him for his lawyer, even bombed. He took the rap and the muscle for providing the pleasures that had been allowed to Harlem and permitted to take place behind the wall of the ghetto. In return, his community honored him as a leader among men and paid balm for his wounds.

There had been only silence to Shaft's opening savagery.

'Did you hear me, you overgrown pimp?'

'I hear you.'

The great rumble, but with the emptiness of out-of-tune kettle drums.

He talked. Persons heard him.

Shaft watched the iron-fenced center strip of Park Avenue roll by after they came across Forty-ninth Street and turned south. Each block was jammed with tulips. Each section another shade. Red, white and red, yellow, deep purple. Carefully planted spotlights allowed the flowers no rest, but caught them and held them as brilliant splashes of spring color. Somebody's rich widow gave them to the city. Shaft remembered reading about it in the *Times*. But he couldn't quite understand it. What the hell good were they as window dressing on a city like this? It was a money city. They should plant rows of sticks with hundred-dollar bills tied to them to show what it all meant and stood for: the cat who has the bread is The Man. The cab rolled into the tomblike arch and up the ramp around the sterile ugliness of the Pan Am Building and grubby Grand Central Station. In the darkness, he wondered fleetingly about the man who screwed the world out of the price of tulips in the first place. Maybe he didn't even like tulips . . . and look what his money was doing now. And maybe he, John Shaft, was freaking out. Crazy. Crazier than Anderozzi knows. Goddamn, he had to get rid of it, waste it. He couldn't even think.

Shaft considered calling her from the YMCA lobby phone. But he was too impatient. He rode the elevator to the sixth floor, showed the sleepy, slow attendant his membership card and got a thin, institutional towel. It wouldn't dry the ass of an emaciated midget, he thought, questioning the logic of a place so involved in wetness from the pool, the showers, the steamrooms yet so dedicated to skimpy towels. Walking back to the locker room, he caught a glimmering insight into the sourness the day was squeezing out of him.

'Keep it up, man,' he said aloud, 'and about six cats in white coats will come running out of Bellevue to throw nets over you.'

Tension did that. So did anger. That's why he was here. There were two or three paunchy, bald, Jewish business types in the locker room. There were a lot of wholesale fabric dealers in the area and they stopped for a steaming and rub just as their richer cousins did at the flossy midtown health clubs. No one he knew. He had a nodding acquaintance with only two or three of the other people who came to the place for whatever reason. It wasn't his club. It was his escape hatch, decompression chamber. The thought of the lanky man skating across the floor and out the window nagged him for a second. Fuck it, go away. The vision fled.

Shaft felt the dampness touch his body as he stripped and began hanging his clothes in the thin slit of a locker. His body almost always felt good. He knew its value, from the first beating it had survived, from the first club-swinging cop it had outrun through a trash-cluttered alley, from the first concrete chasms it had leaped between Harlem tenements, from the bullets it had survived. Shaft glanced at the scars, circular puckers of indented flesh on his left side. Two in the meaty muscle of the upper thigh, the third in the lower left abdomen. The last one surrounded by the slice and stitch marks of surgery. Maybe it was the pressure of people coming after him with guns again, maybe it was looking at the scars again, but the memory of how he got them went through his mind. He saw the Vietcong teenager's wan, weary face peering out of the bunker south of Danang. Peering over the brush-covered length of a rifle that was almost bigger than the kid. Bing, bing, bing. Like that. He had three holes in his left side, he was spinning on his own ankles like a wobbling top and the impartial judgment of his own automatic rifle was somehow chewing its way toward the surprised almond eyes. The medics told Shaft he should have died on the deck of the helicopter that carried him out of the place where his blood had joined the jungle ooze. They told him he should have died at the first medical station of his unit. But they told him he was one tough sonofabitch who was going to live when the base hospital surgeon finished the hurried, harried work of relinking his intestines. Shaft shook the vision from his head as he pulled on the jock strap and the sweatsuit. He jogged out of the locker room and took the stairs to the workout room two at a time, a dead run at a forty-five-degree angle up. He had work to do.

'Ye-es.' The word came through the apartment intercom in two syllables. 'What is it?'

'John Shaft.'

The catch release on the glass-and-wood door buzzed and he pushed into the hallway of the old brownstone on West Twenty-first Street. He had gone around the slanted track of the McBurney gym again and again, swung hand by hand on the overhead ladder like a demented, driven Tarzan, rowed a mighty river on a machine that never moved, and gotten up to run again . . . until the sweatsuit slopped around his ankles as a mushy bag of the perspiration pouring out of him, his heart thundered against the walls of his chest with a threat to explode into shrapnel of flesh and his breathing was a hoarse scream. He quit because he had to, stood trembling in the burning rain of the shower and then plunged into the pool to let the water lift and lave the muscles he had tried. He had to be with her then: he could not conceive she would not be there.

'John,' she used his name. 'John.' It was a soft cry, more relief than welcome. 'I read about you. There was something on the seven-o'clock news about that man in . . .'

'Shhhh.'

She was herself now. The tangerine wig and the purple coat were in the closet. She was a tall, slim girl whose light brown hair drifted in a whispering haze toward her shoulders. An almost pretty girl who was instead beautiful, whose lean features had made him think of English movies when they met, whose body was wrapped now in a bright blue Japanese man's robe that barely touched her thighs.

'Shhhh,' Shaft quieted her, reading and folding her into his arms, burying his face in the soft, fine hair beneath her right ear and filling his lungs with the jasmine scent of the Guerlain soap she used.

'I worried.'

'Don't.'

'But I . . .'

His mouth closed on hers and stopped the words. His hands moved across her back, feeling the muscles and tendons beneath the firm flesh. His cheek also felt the touch of something that could have been a tear from her blue-gray eyes, or the moisture from the scrubbing that had taken away the day's make-up and made her face pale white, fresh and shining. She filled his hands with vibrancy, movement as she pressed against him, her hands holding his face, stroking his neck and tracing fire across his shoulders.

'Ellie, baby,' he gasped when their mouths tore apart and he sank his head to the nuzzling place on her throat and her head fell back, her eyes closed. She was talking to him with her body, speaking to him from pelvis to the small round breasts against the flat slab of his torso. He was answering, demanding.

He felt her hands move across his shoulders and down his chest, forcing their way between them, opening the button of the gray suit, moving inside to the warmth of his chest and then lower to the robe's belt and the clothes that were between them. She was nibbling his ear, biting him, licking, kissing and urging him.

'You are so warm,' she said. 'The heat of you. The heat of you.' She began to croon it, murmur and moan it. Her arms were wrapped around his neck and he felt her legs rise and entwine themselves on his, leaving the holding of her to the strength of his hands and arms. In a sudden freedom and finding Shaft entered her and pressed her down and down upon his body, an impaled figure clinging to the thrust of his need for her. He walked with her that way. They moved together in the single entity of passion, walked to the couch where he laid her gently down and began the rhythmic pulsing of the explosions they contained.

'Oh, Shaft!' she cried out. 'Fuck me! Fuck me!'

An hour. Two hours. The time drifted away as gently as old fog. He smoked one of her Parliaments and looked from the wide, long bed toward the window of the apartment. The shutters were partially open and slits of light and darkness broke the solid shape of the wall. He was thinking about the way she had moved to meet his thrust. He was thinking of getting dressed and leaving.

'I want to sleep against your warm body,' she said, very sleepily, very quietly. 'I want to hold you there and to go to sleep with you in my hand.'

There was an Episcopalian seminary across the street, its beacons of purity casting the lights against the blinds, lights for the new crop of spokesman of some god he knew did not exist and had very little to say that he could understand. He wondered what the seminarians would say if they could see these bodies side by side, hear her words. They would strangle in their little white collars.

'I'll try to be back. A man is coming to my office to see me at midnight. I'll try to get back as quick as I can.'

She had to understand and, if she couldn't understand, she had to accept. He couldn't pour it all out and try to explain why he must be there for the meeting with Knocks Persons. She just had to take it. Maybe that message was there in the way he had spoken.

'Whenever you're done. Wake me up.' She put her cheek against his shoulder and went to sleep. He did not move until she was deeply into it, gone from the world he lived in.

Chapter Three

KNOCKS DIDN'T. He opened the door without a sound and rolled into the office as quietly as a coasting locomotive. And almost as big. They had agreed on midnight. It was midnight. Shaft was impressed that anything, anybody, so huge could move so quietly. It was an art form in the world where menace was your neighbor who came knocking at odd hours to borrow a cup of blood. But it was an art in which the masters were usually small, tight men, set closely upon the ground they wished to cover. Shaft knew that he couldn't do it. He was fast, faster than almost anyone he knew, and strong, stronger than almost anyone he had tried. But he wasn't quiet. He envied Persons the capacity of it.

That was all he felt as the black giant of Harlem racketeering made one of the straight-back wooden chairs disappear by lowering the hulk of his body upon it. There was an overpowering sense of authority about the man, but no threat to Shaft. Persons wouldn't be there on the chair, wouldn't have tolerated his call or the killing of the intruder that morning, if he did not want Shaft alive for one reason or another. Now what was it?

'You alone?' Persons asked.

'I'm alone.'

He did not have to ask about Persons. Somewhere in the night, in the dregs that remained after the theatergoers had been poured out of Times Square, were Persons' men. In the hallway, on the street, probably even in the fire alley behind the building. Persons was like a Pope or a king; he could never be alone in his lofty eminence. Too many people wanted him or something he had.

Shaft looked for Persons' eyes, which were tucked away in folds of flesh. So we all look alike, do we? The head of the man was shaven, glistening, the jaw around the full, firm mouth was heavy-boned and hard. Nature had structured Knocks Persons to drive through immovable objects and beat back irresistible forces.

'I got you mad without us ever meeting,' Persons said. 'That was a mistake. Mine.'

'A lot of people I never met make me mad.'

'You so mad you couldn't work for me?'

'If it pays and you're coming in here like any other client, I don't get that mad.'

'It pay. And that's how I'm here.'

'Okay, what do you want?'

Shaft still couldn't find the man's eyes. They lurked there beneath the heavy ridge of skull at the start of his forehead, shadowing the area between the brows and the large, appropriately strong nose. But while he wondered, he was relaxed. Confronted with the figure of Persons, his abstract anger was pointless.

'What I want? I want my baby back.'

And Shaft discovered why he couldn't find the eyes. Persons had been squeezing them tight to fight back the tears that now came trickling down the face of the man. Shaft had a feeling of history along with some embarrassment. He was watching an epic event in a sordid context. Knocks Persons, who got his name from the community because he had taken all the knocks and bumps that anybody could give him without stopping or even slowing down, was crying. That surprised Shaft. It shocked him.

'Mr. Persons . . .'

One of the bear paws waved aside the words and plunged into the folds of the black suit for a crisply white handkerchief that seemed to be about the size of a twin bed sheet. Persons wiped away the tears, stuffed the handkerchief away and found a long, green cigar in an inside pocket. The ritual of the cigar fascinated Shaft. He watched Persons strip off the cellophane, remove the band that said Havana Upmann, one of the pre-Castro cigars that are still around in private humidors of the very wealthy. He knew Persons wouldn't bite the end and he was pleased to see a hand dip into the change pocket in his suit and come out with a small gold cigar clipper. Shaft also felt an impulse to lean over with a match and light the cigar. He didn't. Persons wasn't fishing for the gesture. He got his own matches, lighted the Havana and dropped the bit of tobacco and the wrapper into Shaft's ashtray while the curl of smoke rose around his bald head in a carcinogenic halo.

'You a young man, Mr. Shaft,' Persons said. 'But you been aroun'. I'd just as soon you forget you saw that.'

Shaft nodded. He'd never forget it. But he'd never mention it. He knew the price of pride.

'You know me and you know what I do. Maybe you even know my baby.'

It was a question. Shaft knew Persons had a wife since he had talked with Anderozzi about the pay telephone in the closet. But he didn't know Baby. Was it a showgirl Persons was keeping? The old bastard looked up to it.

'No, I don't know Baby.'

'Maybe you do but don't know she's mine. She don't often admit to me. I don't say anything about her. She use her mother's name mostly. Beatrice Thomas is what she call herself. But she's mine.'

Shaft's memory circuit made no connections to the name.

He was about to jot it down on the legal pad at the right of his desk blotter, but stopped himself. Not with Knocks Persons. Write nothing down. Give them nothing to read about what you know, what you do. He tapped his teeth with the ballpoint instead.

'I don't understand. Is this a girlfriend of yours?'

There was pride as well as concern in the rumble.

'Beatrice is my daughter. Even if she don't like to admit it. She's my baby.'

She was nineteen now. A pretty one, from what Knocks saw of her and what they told him about how she looked. She had grown up so fast. And so furiously. Why, Knocks said, he could remember when she actually was a baby, not like he just called her that now. About as big as a button when she was born and she never seemed to be wanting to grow much bigger. In those early days, Knocks Persons remembered, he could almost hold her in one hand. He had been holding her, in fact, when the law came busting through the door and said he had to go away with them for questioning. He got back five years later and she was a sassy, bright little girl easily frightened by strangers. Baby was going to school with the nuns and her name was Beatrice Thomas because that's what her mother said it was.

'No little girl of mine going to school with no jailbird name on her,' she said.

But she was his little girl, too, wasn't she?

'Not anymore, Mr. Persons,' she had said. 'You got your business and your po-leece and your jails and there's no room in that for a little girl like her.'

Maybe that woman was right. Maybe she wasn't. But the day she told him, he left their apartment just east of Amsterdam Avenue to go back to repairing the battlements of his empire. He turned the ignition key and saw the front end of his new

Coupe de Ville disappear in a roar that left him deaf for two days, bleeding for three, dedicated for all time to having a chauffeur turn the key for him.

If that was the way it was going to be, little Beatrice Thomas had probably best go on being just that.

There were many things to do for Knocks Persons as he took control of the policy racket, the bookies, the floating action for the high-rolling crapshooters, the hustlers and the men who hustled them. He even went so far as to take one of the women, a beautiful light-skinned dancer, under his widening sphere. But there was only one baby. He kept further away from her than he did from legality. He sent money, clothes, presents and he even saw that her mother's companions were respectable, gentlemanly, abstemious – and terrorized of saying or doing the wrong thing in the girl's presence.

Once a week, he went into the closet to pick up the phone and get a dime's worth of information about Baby. It was all he could stand.

She was fourteen, he said, when she learned who she was and what he wasn't. The words that described him were only on the periphery of her vocabulary as a child guided carefully through the ghetto streets to parochial schools, her mother's idea of the best possible insulation. But Beatrice was smart and learned their meaning quickly. With it, she discovered that she was just an upper middle-class Negro girl whose widowed mother had investments that supported them. Not just a girl faced with the identity conflicts of the place and time in which she found herself. She was the child of the worst of men . . . and even he had rejected her.

'She just went wild,' Persons said. 'She wouldn't go back to school. Too shamed. Her mama tell me she wouldn't even talk. Just cry or look out the window.'

All his presents failed to touch the hidden horror of her

discovery, which had come as simply as a schoolmate's bit of teasing. Her mother's entreaties failed, too. A visit from the monsignor in charge of her school evoked only hysterical weeping.

'I finally went to see her myself. I had to. She screamed when I told her who I was. She screamed a lot of things. The only one that made any sense was she kept calling me the devil, devil, devil. Over and over. And when I couldn't look or listen anymore, she said one more thing. She said she was going to join me in hell.'

She did. By the time she was sixteen, Beatrice was known in every bar Persons owned and many he didn't. By seventeen, she knew every pusher on his payroll. By eighteen, she had undergone two abortions, the drying-out procedure in private institutions in four different countries. Now she was nineteen.

'And I can't find her,' Knocks Persons said. 'Anywhere.'

It took the big man an hour to complete his doleful recital. Shaft interrupted rarely. Then with a simple question.

'Where'd that happen?'

'Rome.'

'Who was the man?'

'That Brazilian fighter, boy named Luis Pinari or something like that.'

'The one who died in the car?'

Persons would nod. And go on.

His was a business of harsh realities, Shaft knew, and he had the feeling that he was being involved in two private nightmares that had no connection with his life. There was a measure of how far he had come from Harlem in the fact that he had not heard any of this before, none of the underground whispers about the private shame and sorrow of big Knocks Persons. Who the hell had he been talking to, he

47

asked himself? Shit, if she did half of what Persons said she did, he had probably run into her two or three dozen times at parties . . . while he had been pursuing somebody like Ellie. He tried to recall freaked-out-looking Negro girls who had caught his attention. He remembered too many. They were all over the place, like the fat-thighed Bronx bagel babies who shaved off their mustaches on Saturday night and flocked down to MacDougal Street. He had tried a taste of both. Who could remember the faces and the bodies, let alone the names? She could have been one of them.

'You had her watched, didn't you?'

Persons dropped the dead butt of the cigar into the ashtray and reached into the folds of the suit for another.

'As much as I could.'

'That makes her a hard girl to lose track of, even in a crowded city.'

Persons was repeating the ritual of the cigar. It occurred to Shaft that the Havana was about the size of a large corncob. It just looked normal in Persons' hand.

'I thought so, too.' He puffed and looked at the coal end of the smoking length of hawser. 'But there's some places my people don't go.'

'How long has she been out of sight?'

'Two weeks.'

'No word, no hint?'

'Nothing. When I say my people looked, they looked.'

Shaft could imagine every rock in Harlem being turned over. What they must have found along the way! One of those nice, well-meaning social workers once asked him what he wanted to be in the world. 'Alive,' he told her. The only place to stay that way was frequently under one of those rocks at the bottom of the swamp. Survival was a dark place, a black place.

'That's why I sent for . . . that's why I come to you.'

A nineteen-year-old Negro girl in a frenzy of drink, drugs and sex. And beautiful, too. Or so he said. She should be easier to find than a cigarette in Winston-Salem, N.C.

Shaft did not quite understand what had happened between Beatrice Thomas and her father. Persons might have screwed the little girl's head on straight with just one swipe of those huge paws. At least it would have told her that her father was a man – which is more than many little girls in Harlem know about their fathers by the time they are in high school. At least it would have showed her that he cared enough to be hurt by her, so deeply that he had to strike out at her. Shaft also wondered why the old man had continued to tolerate the relationship of pain and punishment between himself and his daughter. Why hadn't he just cut her off? Persons should have been capable of that. He was probably harder, inside and out, than anyone Shaft knew or cared to know. And Shaft considered the possibly fatal course of telling Persons that the best thing he could do was say good riddance to Beatrice, to thank his good fortune that she was gone to whatever private hell she sought out.

Shaft also considered sending Persons on his way. The hate that came with most of his cases, husbands and wives hating husbands and wives, insurance companies hating claims, stores hating thieves, all of that was relatively simple and clear. But this one had too many elements of love to be at all precise and clear in the route from A, the problem, to B, the solution. Beatrice Thomas was bad news. She was not likely to be anything else to John Shaft, investigator of her disappearance, especially since her father, with all his connections and contacts, had not been able to find a trace of her.

'Mr. Persons, the first thing that an honest private detective has got to tell you is that the best place to go right now is to the Missing Persons Bureau of the New York Police Department. They know who's been carried into the hospitals . . . who's been carried into the morgue. With them, it's a system, something they do every day. If anything has happened to Beatrice they'll know about it. Next, if you push them a little to find out if she has been seen, who she's been seen with, and if there is anything to follow in that direction . . .'

Shaft let the words trail off. He must be out of his mind suggesting that Knocks Persons go to the police. All Persons had to do was lift the corner of the carpet and he'd find the police sitting there taking notes. Listening. Watching. He would get about as much sympathy from them, as much help and understanding as a housewife wastes on a bedbug swimming across a clean sheet. The police had been trying to get Knocks Persons in a vulnerable position for three decades. They would only welcome this discomfort and possibly attempt to use it. No, he knew Persons couldn't go to the police. Knocks knew it, too. That's why he was there with Shaft.

'I tell you, Mr. Shaft. I tell you, if there was another way, I'd go. The last thing I want is somebody, anybody, anywhere poking around my business. And it's all right for you to sit there and think it shouldn't matter that much, that I should just go on my way, do what I have to do while the little girl is gone. Well, it don't matter. It don't matter who understands. All I know is now that she's gone like this, I can't think of anything else and I can't do anything else except try to get her back. Get her back where I can kind of watch over her in my own way, until she gets all this straightened out. And you. You're a black man. Somewhere inside of you you know what this girl's feeling and what she's thinking. But you're also part a white man because of what you do and where you been. And you smart enough to go back and forth between black and white man. That's what I'm asking you to do. I want you to think for me about this little girl and I want you to go back and forth between being a black man and a white man, and find her for me. It ain't going to hurt you none. And I got some ways to make it help you a whole lot to do that for me.'

Shaft had been called many things, even Tom by some belligerent separatists. He had never been called a white man before. But he knew. Persons, so black in his own way, understood the dichotomy. And, yes, Persons also had many things he could do for Shaft. Most of them had Benjamin Franklin's picture engraved on them and were stuffed into his wallet. Yet Shaft felt uneasy about becoming involved with Persons. It was a healthy attitude. Persons was an impossible man to control. He was a figure standing alone on a foundation of corruption. His identity could become part of Shaft's identity, at least in the eyes of the police with whom Shaft dealt. Yet his power would also become part of Shaft's power. Realistic about its seductive quality, wary of the chains, he was fascinated by the idea. He was also intrigued by the idea that Beatrice could disappear and all the king's men couldn't find her. Could he? Why not? Better than they could, he could do what was necessary.

'If I decide to give it a try, I need two things from you.'

'How much?'

'Not money yet. We'll get to that in a minute. What I need is your promise that there won't be any more shit like this morning, with you sending people after me. People with guns. If I work for you I'll work for you, and you'll get the same straight, ethical deal that any other client gets when he walks into this office. But there can't be anybody behind me or waiting in front of me where I can trip over him or have him mess up my play. I'll just tell you right now if you ever send anybody after me again I'm going to kill the motherfuckers and then come looking for you.'

The old man didn't even blink his hooded yellow eyes. He may even have nodded slightly in agreement. Shaft wasn't sure.

'The other thing is you have to tell me the truth about everything I ask. It's never going beyond this room or this head but I have to know everything I can that seems necessary to doing this thing whether you want to tell me or not. I won't write anything down and nobody'll know that I know. And it may seem crazy to you that I *want* to know. But it's part of it. It's one of the tools of the job. It's one I have to have if I'm going to do it right.'

Persons might well have been disturbed at the suggestion that he would have to open some of the dark corners of his mind to Shaft's probing as the price of regaining communication with his daughter. But he did not debate it very long. He looked at Shaft in silence for a few moments and dispensed with the matter, moved on to the next.

'How much money you want?'

How much money did Shaft want? It was a beautiful question. He wanted *all* the money. He wanted every fucking penny that had been minted or printed. He wanted all the money he could possibly use. All the money he could luxuriate in. Knocks Persons had it and Shaft could probably get at it. It wasn't like any other case. These weren't real people. Goddamn. There was only one way to go. There never was more than one way to go, even now.

'My rate will figure to be about twelve dollars an hour, which is about the average. Maybe a little under the average for a private eye in New York. You'll have to take my word for all expenses. What I mean when I say expenses is if I have to rent a car, I'm just going to go ahead and do it without worrying about it. When I do it's on a twenty-four-hour basis and maybe I'll have to abandon the damn thing someplace and there'll be a charge for bringing it back to the garage. Things like that. If I have to buy information for a hundred dollars or so, I'm going to have to use my own judgment on how much it's worth and how badly we need it. Beatrice has been a lot of fancy places. If I have to go there for one reason or another, I have to go there first class. That's part of the expenses. I can't go anywhere looking like a cop and it may cost a few dollars keeping me from looking like one . . .'

Knocks interrupted him. 'I don't care about any of that,' he said, reaching into the left inside pocket of his coat for a fat yellow envelope. He flipped it casually, with hardly a movement of his huge body, onto the desk blotter in front of Shaft. It was casual, but it was not insulting. Just the Persons way. 'When that's gone, you let me know what you need.'

Shaft picked up the envelope, hefted it for a moment in his right hand and frowned at it. He considered opening it, writing Knocks Persons a receipt in the customary manner and putting its contents aside for deposit in his bank account. But that would not be to Persons' liking, writing numbers and names on paper. There was enough there. There would always be enough there when Persons stuffed the envelope. Shaft stuck it into his own coat, feeling it bulge and nestle against the flat muscles of his chest. It felt even larger there than it had in his hand. It probably made him look as if he were carrying a cannon, a piece, heat.

'All right,' he said. 'When that's gone I'll let you know. Now I need some facts. Without emotion. Now I need the truth.'

Shaft was starved. The fact that he had not eaten struck him when he walked out of the building and into Times Square. The glitter of Persons' Cadillac limousine, a black Fleetwood, had already vanished among the sequins of the night. It was another sparkling dot among a million or two just like it, somewhere speeding the big man back to his castle.

Damn, but he was hungry. He barely looked at the worn wax faces that Times Square was wearing. He wanted a hot dog.

He also wanted to sleep. He turned south toward Forty-third Street and Benedict's stand over on the Seventh Avenue side of the Square. There were three or four hustlers there, a couple of pimply kids with scraggly mustaches, two or three black cats in hip-length black leather coats and bopper hats. They didn't pay any attention to him; he returned the compliment of acceptance.

The orange juice was ice-cold and tasted of rind. The hot dog was hot and tasted of the garlic that had been added to obscure the meat. He had to go to Harlem. He had to go but he didn't want to. Shaft had not really considered the two faces on the coin of his world until Persons had put it to him with the astuteness of his own black identity. Shaft was black, Persons had said, but he was also white. Was he, really? His world was both worlds. He wondered how well he had made the transition and, in fact, what changes had come to him that made it so simple for Persons to label him a mutation. He had to go to Harlem. He had to go find some of the people who hated Knocks Persons and ask them just how badly they hated.

'That's a dollar ninety, mister.'

'A dollar ninety for what?'

'That's seven hot dogs at twenty cents a hot dog and fifty for orange juice.'

'What seven hot dogs?'

'Mister, you ate seven hot dogs.'

Seven hot dogs? Shaft felt the bulge of his stomach muscles at the belt. He had been standing there thinking and apparently he had gorged on seven of the long red cylinders of meat and miscellany off the greasy grill. Seven hot dogs. That was pretty good. For a second, he felt rather proud of himself. He was full but he wished he could remember eating them. He handed the nervous Puerto Rican counterman two dollars.

'Okay,' he said, 'what's so unusual about seven hot dogs?'

The Puerto Rican smiled at him, rang up the dollar ninety. Shaft belched. Whoosh. Seven hot dogs. He wished he could remember eating them. He wondered if people ever actually exploded. He'd never read about it happening.

Chapter Four

BEN BUFORD'S voice was a magnificent thing. It could crackle with the lightning of anger, keen with the sorrow of exhortation and spiritual need, thunder with the depth of profundity and meaning. It was a thing apart from the man, who stood Watusi-tall and warrior-fierce in his stance. So tall and lean with a great bush of tight black curls surrounding his slender ascetic face. His arms and legs so slim and long that even the suits he affected were not quite enough to cloak the angularity of the body. He did not look at all like his voice. A warrior or an inflamed divinity student with gold-rimmed glasses perched on his nose. But when the chorus of his voice sounded, his audiences saw something more than the man who was evident to them outwardly. They heard and saw the man who was there in Detroit when it was burning, in Watts when it was burning, in Bedford-Stuyvesant when it was burning. They heard and saw the man who was out front for them when the time came to light the fires, to pick up the guns, to go to the rooftops, and let it happen. And Buford knew exactly what he was, too, what the voice meant, and what he meant.

There were four men with him in the room over Amsterdam Avenue in the middle ground of Manhattan. Three of them were very much like himself. Tall, perhaps a little more muscular, crowned with the black Afro-bushes of hair. Stern, pure, intense. The fourth was a short, flashily dressed black man whose hair was straight, pomaded, whose suit was Italian, and whose shoes were sixty-dollar alligator loafers. He was frightened and he wasn't sure why. The police didn't frighten him. The Narcs didn't frighten him. His own customers (who were capable of killing a man for a lot less than he usually carried) didn't frighten him either. But Ben Buford did. The tall angular man who had suddenly pointed a long bony finger at his face, the voice that was now thundering at him:

'Goddamn you, you motherfucker! I'm dying for you! Now you get your ass out of here and you get me what I need and you get it back here by four o'clock. That's when I need it. You go!'

Frightened, still not sure why he was frightened, he got up to leave the room.

'I'm going to try, Ben. I'm going to try.'

His assurance was as shaky as the knotted muscles in his gut.

'You try. You do that. You get back here by four.'

The man left. The eyes of the others were on Buford. They watched his frozen mask of authority melt into a smile. 'You want to bet he gets back here with the shit?' They smiled. It was no bet. The man, the pusher, would be back and would have what Ben Buford needed and wanted before he set off again on another of his tours through the country.

Ben took a chair at the head of the battered red maple table that was just about the only furniture in the small, drab room. The others took places around him. They did not defer too obviously. It was much too cool for that, but when he moved they also moved – about half a second afterward, always to a place just a few inches behind or below. He was the leader, they were the corps. This was the Revolution.

'What did the lawyer say?'

'He want you to call him, Ben.'

'What the hell for?'

'He says you probably got to go down to Atlanta and go to court yourself this time.'

'Shit.'

'Maybe it's not so bad, Ben, you could hit maybe six, eight, even ten schools along the way. The brothers need to hear you, to see you.'

That was Lonnie Dotts. Always pushing him into the clutch of some fool students who thought the barricades were made of books, thought they were going to drown Whitey in their cans of beer, figured they could back his play just by listening, yelling, crying out, 'Tell it like it is, Ben!' It was a drag. It was better here in the ghetto. Here they knew what it was all about. They lived with it. It ground them down. They paid the fucking dues just to stay alive. It wasn't an intellectual adventure; it was the bed-bugs that got you in the night and the garbage stink that singed your nostrils in the heat of day. Atlanta. That judge wanted to send his ass to jail as soon as possible, as long as possible, as legal as possible.

'Cat's coming up here to see me.'

The others looked a little surprised. They had had the room only four days. They had been convinced that no one knew of it or that Ben Buford was using it. That was the scheme. Three days here, four days there, never sit still. Keep finding places for Ben. Keep the FBI moving, keep the CIA moving, keep Ben moving, all in different directions. Sometimes he needed a good rest and women. They would check into a Statler-Hilton for four or five days without any attempt to hide. Then he could meet the press, give interviews, get his picture taken, talk to the magazine people, do everything in a big, flashy, public way. So everybody would know he wasn't trying to hide and that he was really out front. Then he would disappear back into the little rooms, ever changing but always the same, with a few rickety pieces of furniture, a raw bulb glaring out of a dangling socket that hung like a noose from the aged, stained ceiling. This was where the work was done.

The three young men sitting with Ben Buford were his praetorian guard, his administrative council, his friends and the very closest of his associates. Longford Dotts, who was called the Minister of Information. Beyman Newfield, his program director. Preston Peerce, who was known as field secretary of the organization and who spoke for Ben Buford when he wasn't there. His second in command. They had locked themselves together into a struggle they called the Revolution and were inseparably bound by the consequences of the decision. Actually, they did not trust each other very much in general and, specifically, his three associates did not trust Ben Buford and he was not entirely open with them. They were all working on the knowledge that messiahs come and go with frequency in revolutions. This one, a small fire attempted in a heavy rain, used them like stick matches. Each one striking a brief flash of fire before it sputtered out and grew cold. Buford could see ambition in the others, ambition and envy. They could see something of the same in him although not much of the envy. He held the chair and had the presence. It was a clear unmistakable stamp, that capacity of Buford's to express authority and leadership. He worked with it, used it and had been uplifted by that recognition when he spoke to the sea of faces in a university audience. He had the presence, he was the man and they had no alternative at the moment. Buford had said he would die for them, for all of them. He meant it, to stand with him meant the same aspiration for the rest of them. That was the price of the revolutionary's power. Those were the dues and you paid them.

'Who's this cat coming up here?' Lonnie Dotts asked.

'Told you. Cat I used to know.'

How Buford had arranged the meeting was unknown to

them. He had stopped in a pay telephone booth about two or three hours earlier and made about fifteen or twenty calls, a number of them long distance. He had told them of some of the calls he had made, some of the arrangements he had agreed to. But he had not told them of all the calls and not the ones that had arranged his meeting with John Shaft. In this spotted, stained center of their struggle it was not the place of a follower to ask the leader what he did not care to divulge. They just looked at him and tried to pry it out of him with the hard pressure of their eyes. They failed.

How could the leader of a revolution explain that he had called his mother from the barricades – or that he called her every night and told her not to worry. Fuck the CIA, the FBI, the NSA and all their phone bugs.

'Ben?' Her voice was warm and full of pride. 'Ah almos' forgit to tell you. 'at nice Johnny Shaft you used to play with, he called here lookin' for you. He say he have to talk with you. He such a nice boy. I 'member how you and he always together. He say he ridin' around in a taxicab lookin' for you 'cause he got to find you about somethin' important. I knows you wouldn't min' my tellin' him you was in town.' She paused, uncertain of his reaction. He said nothing. 'I guess you wants to see him as much as he wants to see you, bein' as how you two was such good frien's. He going to call back in about ten minutes. Where should I tell him to meet you?'

How, also, could he tell his mother that he no longer had any friends? Being gone, being in the papers all the time, calling at these crazy hours. That was enough for her. She knew of no revolution. He gave her the address to give John Shaft. And damned the smart motherfucker to a private hell for knowing him so well. But what the hell did he want? Shaft had no business with them. Shaft was . . . what? Shaft was one of the opportunists, the bastards who could hustle both sides of the street. Now *there* was a sonofabitch who couldn't be trusted. Shaft was a pimp for the whores of whiteness. And smart. He would have to be careful. More careful than with Lonnie Dotts, Beyman Newfield, or Preston Peerce, who were ready to crack open those crates, take the pieces and go to the rooftops to die with him.

The object of Buford's anger and suspicion was at that moment asleep. Shaft lay jammed into the rear right corner of a battered taxicab rolling up Amsterdam Avenue past the empty shells of streets. He was wedged into the corner, his legs out along the seat, and across to the other side behind the back of the driver, his head askew, bent to one side against the glass, the chin down on his chest. Shaft pouted when he slept. He looked like a truculent nine-year-old squeezing his eyes shut in protest. But not to the driver of the cab. To him, Shaft was a menace, a nut spade he'd picked up in Times Square and wished he had never seen.

The cab rolled up one of the last hills of Washington Heights at the north end of Manhattan past Yeshiva University and came to a stop at the corner of 198th Street, where the driver paused under a street light, turned to Shaft and puzzled over the sleepy Negro for a moment.

'Hey, buddy.' He said it pretty loud. He didn't have to. Shaft's eyes were open the moment the rhythm of the cab's movement along the shattered pavement of Amsterdam had stopped. He was awake and completely aware. But he didn't move. He didn't want to frighten the cab driver any more than he already had. The meter showed $6.35.

'This One hundred ninety-eighth and Amsterdam?'

'That's right, buddy. This is where you wanted to go.'

Relief in the cabbie's voice. Maybe the spade would get out here. Maybe the black man would go away without robbing him and he could go back to hustling short hauls in Times Square and the upper East Side and maybe a trip to La Guardia or Kennedy, and he could just forget about going into neighborhoods like this at this hour of night with a black passenger. What the hell did he pick him up for, anyway? He could kick himself in the ass.

Shaft wasn't going anywhere. He caught a piece of light shining into the cab from the blue street arc and held it on his watch. Three o'clock. Still an hour. He could still use more sleep. 'How long do you think it would take to get from here down to Battery Park and then back to One hundred thirty-ninth Street and Amsterdam?'

'Oh, come on, mister, is this some kind of game? You want to just go for a ride why don't you take a bus?'

'Too much light. You think it would take an hour?'

'What?'

'Driving to Battery Park then back to One hundred thirty-ninth and Amsterdam?'

'It would take about an hour.' Resigned. He was going to Battery Park. He wondered if this character would hold him up down there or wait until they got back to Harlem. Should he risk his life attempting to attract the attention of a cop, or just go along quietly and attempt to hide his watch under the seat along the way?

Shaft felt a little sorry for the driver. He was an inoffensive man in most ways except that he was a Jew. Shaft could reason about the Jews and he knew full conviction what his reason told him, but he still did not like them. They were in his Harlem childhood, in the candy store, in the clothes store, in the little grocery store, in the little liquor store and in the hock shop. The money store. He hadn't liked them at all in any of those places or the way they had treated him or the way they had treated anyone else. They were the merchants of misery and

62

the feeling would not leave him, no matter how many Jews he now knew and liked. But the cab driver's offense of being Jewish was hardly enough to inspire Shaft's desire to torment him. He disliked Jews, but he hated cab drivers. The fact was simply that he had an hour to kill and the back end of the taxicab was the place to kill it. The best possible place he could think of to sleep.

'Okay,' he said. 'First to Battery Park and wake me up so I can see the Statue of Liberty. I want to wave at the old whore.'

'You shouldn't talk like that.'

'I know it. Drive.'

Shaft refolded his arms across his chest and went back to sleep. The driver of the cab sighed, put the car in gear and turned up 199th Street to pick up St. Nicholas Avenue and eventually the West Side Drive. He might as well take a nice ride down the river before the black bastard cut his throat and took his money. He was too preoccupied to notice the black Pontiac sedan that moved behind them and followed through the empty street and the vacuum of the night, carefully but definitely.

It was a long night for Victor Anderozzi. Time lost its continuum for him now and then. He was getting old or getting bored. He would be finishing up a report, come to the point where it demanded the date and the time, and glance at his watch. 'Jesus Christ it's three o'clock in the morning.' A moment ago it was only seven in the evening and he had lost most of the hours in between. He should be grateful for reports that demanded the date and time. It made him keep track, or they kept track of him. Years ago he had wondered about his wife and children in those broken hours of darkness. Now he assumed they were all right or that somebody would tell him if they were not. He felt now as if that part of his life did not exist, as though it had vanished along with the sequence of time. Jesus Christ, it was three-thirty in the goddamn morning and he had to go see the Commissioner of Police. He reached for the telephone.

'Have Charlie get the car. Going downtown.'

What, Anderozzi asked as he pulled on his short, brown raincoat, was a Police Commissioner in a city this size doing out of bed this time of night? He also thought of the answer. He was sitting in his office at that moment, a bald little bundle of melancholia and frustration about his own authority and the thirty thousand men who were supposed to be in his charge, the unrest of the community, and the limits of his capacity to apply one to the other. There were departments within departments, wheels within wheels. Who was actually in charge of the Police Department might be a matter of conjecture from day to day. The Commissioner represented the political control of the department. He spoke for the Mayor. The Mayor spoke for the people. Yet the Mayor represented himself, a man trapped in a sea of urban agony by his ambitions for public office, his current one being the least of them. The Mayor spoke for himself and his ambitions insofar as public acceptability made it possible. Oh, hell, it was all garbage. Anderozzi was annoyed with himself for thinking about it. The cops were for the cops. The politicians for the politicians. The people for themselves. That's how it broke down, pulverized. Everybody for himself. They were all caught in this whole screwed-up period of testing and rejecting authority, of everybody trying to kill his old man in one way or the other. It was no surprise to him that people left the country to go live in France or the Caribbean Islands. He wished he could. It was no wonder so many cops bought chicken farms out in the sticks. They were dismal failures as farmers but at least they had a few years of escape from the constant struggle. He had no escape. He was honest. That would keep him poor. And he hated chickens.

The Commissioner's secretary was there, too. A nice-looking woman of about forty. Jewish. Anderozzi liked dark women. Like his wife. Even the faint shadow of mustache was intriguing, sensual to him. He liked hair. Dark hair. Black hair. Black eyes. He liked this woman.

'Get him a cup of coffee. How do you take it? Black?'

'Black,' Anderozzi said, thinking about the secretary and not the coffee.

The Commissioner was there at four o'clock, she was there at four. She wasn't his secretary; she was his wife, the Jewish mother of them all. Why shouldn't she be there? He needed her, didn't he? Dark women were like that. You needed them, goddamnit, they were there. His wife was like that. She put the old-fashioned white pottery mug down on the coaster in front of him on the edge of the Commissioner's desk. Anderozzi picked it up and let the hot fragrant fumes reach up his hawk-beak nose. He sipped tentatively.

'What does it look like, Vic?' Peering at him over his own steaming mug. The Commissioner had great eyes. They nailed you to the wall. They looked right through you, punching holes as they went. Eyes. He had spikes for eyes. He could cut you with them. Short. Bald. Mean. Tough little sonofabitch.

'I'm not entirely sure this is a race thing,' Anderozzi said, assuming they both knew why the Commissioner had summoned him. 'Not the kind of race thing I've seen before. There's something different.'

'Well,' the Commissioner suggested happily, 'maybe they are off on a little internecine warfare of their own?'

'I'm not sure, but let me tell you what I think and let me tell you what I know. Maybe somewhere between those are the facts that we are working with here. Maybe we'll have

65

some of the answers when City Hall starts throwing some of the questions.'

'I better have *all* the answers.'

'You'll have all that I have.'

'I know that, Vic. I'm sorry. I didn't mean that the way it came out. But I don't want to be the Police Commissioner in a city that has to spray tear gas on the streets from helicopters, where the National Guard is shooting up old broads who are looking out the window to see what is going on. Go ahead and tell me. Tell me what you know, then tell me what you think.'

'I know . . . we know that the militants up there are about six months from being ready. They already have the guns, or they soon will have. The estimates are that at least one hundred weapons a week have been accumulated, stored, made ready at various points over the last four years. I think that estimate is low, very low. Well, at any rate that's the estimate we got. FBI, CIA, NSA. That many guns is a hell of a war. In this city, I'd quit trying to count them. There's plenty to go around. So they have a sufficient number of guns. Ammunition, too. This disappeared in greater variety and amount in the last two years than at any time in history of the records we keep. This is being stockpiled somewhere or the North Vietnamese must have been stealing it.'

'How does it break down?'

'In military terms it's fairly unsophisticated. One third in hand guns, one third in rifles, the remaining third of it in shotguns, grenades, a few bazookas, some machine guns, maybe a mortar.'

'Who the hell will care about military terms when that hits the streets? The day when we react so that we speak in military terms, it's going to be a war, not a community crisis.'

The Commissioner was desperate for a definition of the

problem. Tanks *would* roll down the streets of this town. There *would* be a war, not a shootout.

'What a fucking mess,' the Commissioner conceded.

'Yes,' Anderozzi said. 'Yes.'

'What's the best guess on how much of that can be located? Do we know where it is?'

'We don't. But the others figure they can get about half of it. Pick it up instantly. Grab it, seal it off and blow it to hell and make it unusable. The other half is in mattresses, in the back of television sets, in lamp bases, in the flour cans, in toilet tanks, in the earth, in the walls, in every goddamn place you can possibly imagine.'

They sat for a moment in silence and the Commissioner stabbed angrily at one of the buttons on his desk. The door behind Anderozzi opened silently with a push of air against the back of his neck.

'Get us some coffee, will you, Sylvie?'

'You, too, Lieutenant?' she said, bending over his coffee cup, smiling warmly, subtly, comfortingly.

All the dark ones had that compassion except the screwed-up career ones. But he liked them, too. Just on the basis of the look.

'Me, too.'

'I want to tear out every goddamn room north of Fifty-ninth Street!' The Commissioner slapped a fat little fist down on the blotter top of the big mahogany desk that was once occupied by Theodore Roosevelt, who would have and could have searched every goddamn room north of Fifty-ninth Street.

'You'd need an army for that, too,' Anderozzi remarked.

'Okay. What else do you know?'

'Commissioner, if you don't mind, what the hell are you doing up at four in the morning?'

'I'm up at four o'clock because the goddamn Mayor didn't

get home till two o'clock this morning and decided it was a good time to pick up the telephone and call me. He heard talk at the party where he'd been dancing that things in Harlem were on the way up and he wanted to know what I knew. And he said he wanted to know in detail again in the morning.'

'We also know,' Anderozzi went on, 'that the major problem is recruiting, that they just don't have enough fingers for all those triggers. That's at least one area where we get total agreement from Federal people who give it about six months when everybody figures to be ready, that's when the Muslims, the Panthers, the militants, the whole collection of them will come to a sufficient number of angry, organized and partially trained force to at least attempt a revolution.'

Anderozzi had never said those words before. He had thought them. So had the Commissioner but they never had been said straight without the cloak of euphemism, conjecture, doubt. Having said them, Anderozzi realized how much he believed and had believed them during the months of investigating, probing, attempting to penetrate. He was not afraid; he had been too long in the business for that. But he felt so frustrated and sorrowful at his knowledge of the events to come.

'What kind of informers do you get on a rap like this?' the Commissioner asked, leaning back in the big brown leather chair, his gleaming bald head barely touching the plump top of it.

'The same kind as on anything else. The people who don't want it to happen, the frightened ones, the people who want to be on the side that wins. The rotten ones, the people we plant there. The working ones. The same bunch. The same ones you get on anything else.'

'All right, now tell me what you think.'

'I think we're lucky to have made a connection with Shaft, as tenuous as it may be.'

'He's that spade private eye?'

'Yes, he's that spade private eye. He's also a kind of friend of mine and a very ruthless, ambitious guy. I put a lot of faith . . . or maybe I put sixty or seventy per cent faith in the information he'll give. What I also think,' Anderozzi said, 'is that this thing is more racket than racial. I mean it's more *our* problem, strictly a cop problem, than we think it is. More our problem than a social one.'

'Why?'

'Knocks Persons. He doesn't figure to be the focal point or even a peripheral figure of anything racial.'

'Why not? He's rackets. But he's black. And anything black is racial now.'

'Agreed. But he's never been involved in anything that so much as suggested that he wanted to change Harlem, or the white community, or anything else. His whole life, his whole world is built on the attitudes that made the opportunity for him to function. If anything, Persons would have to be a reverse racist. He probably has a deeper appreciation of the status quo than Lester Maddox or George Wallace. He couldn't prosper in anything but a tight black community, with its corruptible white cops on the take, and the whole feeling that it's all right to go ahead and do those black things like shoot craps, drink gin, play the numbers, just so you do them on that side of the line. So his presence negates the racial angle. At least to me.'

'But you don't know what is involved and what isn't.'

'No, not yet, but if Knocks is part of a threat to bloody up the street it would figure that somebody is trying to take something away from him, to crack open that tight little community of crap shooters and gin drinkers.'

The red telephone on the desk began to ring. The hot line. The Commissioner's hand streaked out and he scooped it from the cradle and up to his ear with the speed of a frontier gun slinger. 'Talk,' he commanded.

His eyes jumped to Anderozzi and back to the phone box as he listened. There was another phone just like that beside the Commissioner's bed. Their only caller was epic disaster in all the forms of it New York contains. The Commissioner listened for a minute and said exactly one word: 'Right.' He dropped the receiver back on the red plastic box and looked at Anderozzi with a grim smile of a man who might be watching his own funeral procession go by.

'So much for conjecture. There's a gun battle going on at One hundred thirty-ninth and Amsterdam and they're fighting it with machine guns.'

Anderozzi felt gray all over like a bag of unemptied vacuum dust. He almost forgot to put down the Commissioner's coffee cup as they hurried out of the room together.

Shaft got to the building at about four o'clock, just as he had figured he would. It was a long drive down to the Battery and back. Now this place was about what he had anticipated. A scabrous slattern of a building, held together with an old mortar of dirt and decay, propped up by the buildings on each side, both in the same clutch of disrepair. Some of the windows had been covered over with sheets of tin and were blank gray eyes on the night. A few of the uncovered frames held no glass and were just wind holes for the swirling puffs of soot that would drift in from the incinerators in better buildings of the area. But people lived behind some of the windows, if you could call them people and if you could call that living. For Harlem, Shaft thought, you could call it the lower middle class. Ben Buford was on the fifth of the five floors in there behind the last door down the dark hallway toward the rear.

He flashed almost immediately on the three – or was it four? – shadow figures in the darkness of adjacent doorways. Fools! Anybody who knew enough to look would pick up on them. They were about as inconspicuous as he might be at a Ku Klux Klan meeting in Biloxi. Why didn't they get up in the blank windows? Were they guarding Buford or advertising his presence? Or trying to get arrested as loiterers? Shaft gave no sign of spotting them. He waited for the frightened cab driver to get out of sight, then sauntered slowly across the street toward the entrance he had been told to seek.

Shaft had anticipated the look of the place. Buildings like it . . . they had been his life until he had gone to soldier, not so much because Uncle Sam wanted him but because a Juvenile Court judge and a probation officer wanted to get rid of him. He had lived in these buildings, slept in them, hidden in them, fled through them, lobbed the missiles of street warfare from their parapets. He remembered them well. Shaft had never felt nostalgia, at least never for anything of his childhood and youth, although he sometimes had a sad feeling that he thought must be like nostalgia over fantasies or thoughts of things he had not known. He remembered, yet he was still surprised when he went up the chipped concrete steps and pushed open the door that was hanging like a broken arm on the entrance to an unlighted hallway. He was surprised at the smells. He had forgotten their assault waves against the senses. You never got that in Scarsdale, Greenwich, Westport, or in any of those little towns out on the Island like Jericho. You didn't even get it in Manhattan unless you stumbled over a slum en route from antiseptic home to air-conditioned office.

Urine. That was dominant. The peculiar, soft, mushy smell of rats. Nesting, mating, scrabbling through the plaster. Age. Age has a rotten tone. Blended with dust and the smoke of old fires that may have eaten away at mattresses or the insulation

71

on wiring or just the debris of paper and garbage in the corners of the basement. Finally, fear. Fear had an aroma, a light but pungent scent that pinched the sinuses as well as the spirit. How could he have forgotten all that when he had lived with it so long?

Shaft went up the broken-back stairwell slowly, carefully. Somewhere above him there was a light, a single bulb glimmering into all this treachery of decay. Only the barest flicker of it reached him. He could not even see his own feet in the murk. They found their way up the stairs. Shaft avoided putting weight against the banister and tried to avoid brushing against the wall. When he stumbled on a loose board and his foot went through the backing that was missing from one tread he grumbled half aloud: 'Why in the fuck *don't* they burn them down?'

He went to the recollection of an old corner friend named Jimmy who had harassed the white cop on the beat along 125th Street between Lenox and Fifth. Jimmy went to the cop every day panhandling for just a penny. 'Gimme a penny, gimme a penny, gimme a penny,' he would chant. 'Why?' the cop asked once and only once. 'Why do you want a penny, Jimmy?'

'Penny buy some matches, penny buy some matches.'

Shaft smiled in the darkness. That door should be it.

He considered giving the door a solid whack, a blow against the nerves of Ben Buford and his people. But he wasn't sure how edgy they would be. They had been bugged and rebugged. Bugged in so many places by so many fools that this might be the moment when somebody answered the door with a .45 or a .30-30. So he knocked. Rap, rap. In the way one neighbor might rap on another's door. It's me, John Shaft, come to borrow a cup of tea. He bet Ben Buford had a cup of tea in there, too. A pound of it, if he had been still long enough to make connections.

Lonnie Dotts opened the door. Shaft did not know him. He saw Ben Buford over Dotts' shoulder. Thinner, more elegant in his clothes than Shaft remembered him. A couple of other figures looking very much like Ben Buford stood with him. Shaft figured he better do the old-friend routine. They all looked suspicious and nervous.

'Hey, man,' he said in Ben Buford's direction. 'How you doing?' Shaft moved into the room without waiting for Dotts to get out of the way. That was the man's choice. He either moved or got trampled. Dotts moved. Shaft was into the room and extending his hand to Buford. 'Hey,' he repeated, smiling widely, hoping without confidence that it was going across sincerely. 'What you been doing?'

Ridiculous. Everybody in the world knew what Ben Buford had been doing. He had been throwing molotovs of words on people, watching them ignite, seeing them explode in the fury of his indictments. Maybe the Florida swamp Indians didn't know what Ben Buford was doing, but that was all.

'I have been doing just fine.' Buford's voice was cold, precise, negative. The hand he permitted Shaft to shake was strong, but there was no warmth or welcome in the grip. There was rage and embarrassment in Buford's eyes. Shaft thought there might also be insanity. Hell, why not? Buford had to be insane to be doing what he was doing, putting himself on the line to get his head blown off. For what? For the Revolution that wasn't going to work in this way, Shaft was convinced, but only in the total and eventual reorientation of a whole society. The other side was just as crazy in its way as Buford was in his. You couldn't bomb it out of them any more than you could shoot it out of Buford.

Shaft marveled at the arrogance of their manner toward him. He wondered what they had read, what homework they had done to gather all that hip shit about revolution they urged on the black proletariat. They weren't going to lead *him* to the barricades looking like that. But they were certainly moving many others. Goddamn if he didn't almost expect Ben Buford's sweet, suffering mother to have a carbine under her mattress. And these cats? They were going to tell her who to burn with it. Shit! He checked out their faces one by one. Hostility. Doubt. Anger. Their clothes were so pretty. Shaft leaned against the widow sill and thought with a twinge of embarrassment that his own suit must look like hell. Like in the morning spilling coffee on himself, and now closing out the night leaning against a filthy window sill about three thousand hours later. In between he had done just about everything but have a dog fight in the gray flannel single-breasted number that came from Paul Stuart's on Madison Avenue. Buford and the others were waiting.

'Listen, all I want is to buy some information about a little girl that's missing,' he said. 'I figure you get around more than most people, so maybe you know this chick or heard about her.'

He was being honest, as honest as a man with three walnut shells. And a round bean. They looked even more suspicious.

'With Whitey's money?' Lonnie Dotts asked. Shaft's threshold of annoyance was about three degrees lower than normal, probably because he was so tired.

'You know,' he said, 'you pretty goddamn stupid.' That was a wet towel across the face. 'The money is green and why in the fuck don't you find out what I'm buying before you say you're not selling?'

Ben Buford came back at him hard with that great voice he threw out at college audiences. 'You can't come up here talking like that, man!'

Shaft wasn't sure he could take all four of them but he was sure he could mess up their clothes, those fine suits, trying to find out. They bored him with all this wasted hostility. He wasn't J. Edgar Hoover. His temper flashed and he sneered: 'Why, you silly mother . . .'

Sound roared up the stairwell with a sudden thunder of doom. There were four or five quick shouts, curses, then the shooting. The choppy prattle of machine-gun fire, just like in the movies. Rat-a-tat-tat. Just like in a war. Pop-pop-pop. The others jumped to their feet.

'Fuck this,' Shaft mumbled. He looked out the window behind him to see if there was anything he could swing from, climb down or hang onto. Nothing but five flights of suicide. They were firing in the stairwell now. More curses. Feet running up the stairs, then stopping. Then more firing. He didn't know how many pieces were in action. But it sure the hell was more than two. That was such a mad sound, such a bad sound. He looked back again. There was still nothing out the window but window. Shit.

He had to get out and take them, too, if he could.

'Where's the heat?' he demanded in a shout. Four heads turned to him, questioning, surprised.

'Where's the goddamn guns?' he roared.

'Got no guns here,' Newfield said.

The silly bastards could run around and get beat up and arrested, smoke a lot of shit, make a lot of noise, but when it came right down to it, and it was coming right down to it this minute, they hadn't figured on how to lay a hand on a decent piece and save everybody's ass from getting shot off. Those people who were coming up the stairs, *they* knew where to get a piece.

'Let's get the hell out of this cigar box!' Shaft commanded, moving toward the door. The door suddenly moved toward him. It flew open with a bang and Shaft was staring into a collection of plumbing that looked like a commando machine gun out of old World War II movies, a piece of pipe, an elbow joint and a clip of .45 cartridges feeding into it. He stopped in mid-movement, hanging over the muzzle on the balls of his feet. Holding the gun in trembling hands was a nineteen or twenty-year-old cat in a leather jacket and black beret. His eyes were wide, near panic.

'Get the hell out of here,' the young man shouted. Shaft wished the kid wasn't using the gun as a pointer, waving it toward the door, passing over his middle on the way.

'What's going on out there?' Buford asked.

'I don't know. They just came in. They wouldn't stop; somebody said stop and they started to shoot.'

'Motherfuckers! Goddamn CIA,' Newfield said.

Shaft checked them out for panic. Ben Buford looked calm enough. His eyes were bugging and his face was filled with anger. But he was calm. Newfield looked scared. Sweat covered his forehead and would soon be rolling around that pudgy face to the black goatee that covered the chin. Lonnie Dotts looked the same but angry. He had the appearance of being permanently pissed off at the world. It wouldn't change if he were buying a pack of cigarettes or if, as now, he was buying a piece of death. The sonsofbitches who were out to get him were all the same and they were everywhere. Preston Peerce, a little shorter, wider than the others, looked more like himself, looked like the most reliable of them. Hooded eyes, showing nothing, not moving, just standing there waiting to decide or for somebody to decide for him what the play should be. There wasn't any time left for thinking. Shaft reached out and grabbed the kid by the shoulder of his jacket, spun him around and said, 'Go, goddamnit!' The kid went out the door, either under his own power or Shaft's push, the gun up and ready to work.

'Let's get the fuck out of here,' Newfield said.

'The roof!' Lonnie Dotts said. 'Up the roof.'

They looked to Buford for a moment. 'Okay,' he said. 'The roof.'

Dotts, Newfield and Peerce ran past Shaft to the door. Buford started out after them. Shaft grabbed him.

'Wait a minute. Wait,' he said. 'Not the roof.'

Buford turned on him, snarling. 'Let go of me, you crazy bastard. We can get over the buildings and the hell out of here.'

Shaft's hand tightened on Buford's arm. Ben would have to tear it out of the socket to get away.

'No, come on.' He virtually dragged Buford out of the room toward the stairs. The gunfire was two, maybe three flights down. And it was one hell of a gunfight, too. The machine guns on and off for both sides were almost a steady roar. But that was the way to go. He started down the stairs pulling the unwilling Buford after him. Buford struggled to free his arm.

'No!' he cried. 'You're taking me down there to get me killed. No!'

Shaft was off balance at the top of the stairs. But he didn't have time to stop and argue. He turned to Buford, let go of his arm with his left hand and turned it into a fist. He brought it up as hard as he could against Ben's chin. Even over all that gunfire, Shaft could hear the crunch of flesh on flesh, bone on bone. Buford's face danced across his skull, his entire body lifted up about an inch and then began to settle. Shaft pulled him forward and caught him over his shoulder. Then with a grunt of exertion he turned down the stairs as quickly as he could move with one hundred seventy pounds of anger over his shoulder.

Ben Buford was his connection into an entire community within a community of the black world Shaft had to prowl to answer the questions that Knocks Persons asked of him. He wasn't going to let that connection go up on an open rooftop to be chopped down like a pigeon. Even if he had to carry Ben Buford through hell he was going to keep the Revolution alive. He started down the rickety stairs.

'Silly sonofabitch,' he muttered.

Chapter Five

THEY HAD the roof figured. They were waiting. Lonnie Dotts died with his arms thrown out as in supplication, a black minor christ nailed to a rusty television antenna with .45-caliber spikes. Half of Preston Peerce's head vanished in that red cloud of the explosion that shattered him. Beyman Newfield was cut through with a line of perforation that looked like a mistake by a giant machine turning out paper people on huge rolls. Two sentries who had tried to prevent this lay lifeless in the street below. But Ben Buford lived. So did John Shaft.

Shaft guessed they had exactly three minutes when the shooting stopped, the footsteps echoed up and then down the stairs. Three minutes for the nearest radio car to get to the building and begin sealing it off. Three minutes to run.

He crawled quickly out from under the sway-backed bed, slithering across the gritty linoleum floor, pulling Buford after him. A spring caught at his suit, near the left shoulder. He swore, jerked hard and tore loose, ripping the fabric. In five seconds, he was out, dragging Buford out, standing up, jerking Buford to his feet by the lapels of the fancy suit. The woman sitting on the bed seemed dazed. She was whimpering in fright and confusion, near hysteria and about to let her mind leap over the edge into a howling abyss of madness. She had been half torn from the stupor of sleep by a gun battle in the hallways of her home. Two men had kicked their way into her apartment. One man had. One was a body. She couldn't even scream, she was too frightened. They were black. And the man had said to just sit and be quiet and it would be all right. They crawled under her bed. The man stuffed the body under her bed and got under there with it. The shooting, all the shooting, it stopped and somebody ran up the stairs and back down again. Swearing. Now they were crawling out from under her bed. It never happened. She was *in* that bed, sleeping, having the worst nightmare of her life. It never happened.

'Come on, goddamnit,' Shaft said, jerking Buford to his feet, slapping the thin, slack-jawed face lightly with his left hand, trying to bring him around. 'Wake up, Ben. We got to run.'

Buford came around. He started to struggle as his eyes bulged open and rolled. Shaft held his arms.

'Stop that shit,' he said. 'You're all right. The party's over. We got to run.'

Buford's anger settled into focus. He oozed hatred. That took twenty seconds.

'No time to argue,' Shaft said. 'I just saved your fucking life. They're gone. Now we got to run. You going to run with me or do I carry you? You got any mother wit, use it, man.'

He was poised to clip Buford again. But Buford heard something in the silence that had returned to the building, something in Shaft's urgency, that pressed harder than his distrust. He nodded. Shaft plunged his left hand into his pocket, came out with a small wad of bills. He dropped them into the woman's lap.

'Try to forget you saw us,' he said. She would want to very much. She never would.

One minute. Move. Run. If they were smart enough to be waiting out there, it was over. If they weren't, it was the only way. He couldn't let the cops have Buford. Shaft spun around from the dazed woman, who was looking down now at the crumpled pile of money in her lap, green against the thin pink fabric of her nightgown. He couldn't worry how Buford followed him now. It had to be now. It was years ago and they were running. They were together, but everybody was on his own. The blue was coming, coming with a scream of sirens and a flash of red to match the blood that might still be spilled. His blood. Buford's blood. Any black blood. Run, goddamnit, run!

Shaft missed about eight of the stairs going down, kicked a corpse stretched out along the railing.

'Watch it there!' he hissed at Buford, skipping the body, barely slowing. He saved those seconds for the doorway. Shaft stopped. The remaining glass was a handful of silvery shards on the floor of the small vestibule. Ragged holes pockmarked the frame. He stopped and looked out. Buford was right behind him, touching him, looking also. The street was empty. But lights were blinking on in the rooms of the tenements across the street. In another minute, heads would come poking out those windows to see what had happened. The streets would fill. The law would be there.

'I'm going out there so goddamned fast nothing can get me,' he whispered. 'Stay with me.'

One great leap. He landed running at the bottom of the snaggle-face concrete steps. Running and crouched. He hoped to hell Buford was in shape, hadn't been standing up to throw so many words that he had forgotten how to run. He landed and was away in a blur of motion. Now nobody could catch him. Nobody could hurt him. This was his way in the world. These dark streets were his place. An exultation of power fed his body from the pit of his stomach. He missed that. He ran, flew. They would find the alley, the doorway, the hidden place in the moment that they needed it. They might be cornered in the rooms of Harlem, but not in the streets. This was really home. His three minutes were up.

Shaft heard the sirens. They were all behind him. Then he saw the pulsating glow of the police car roof flasher lighting the intersection ahead with the throb of its stained-glass brain. The car was running without the siren. He sprang into a doorway, flattened against the shadows and felt more than saw Buford leap in with him. They were breathing hard, sucking wind. The car swept past. They were out of the doorway and running again, close to the building, to avoid so much as a glimpse in the patrol's rear-view mirror. Eyes always looking ahead for the chance cop, the uncommitted squad car. They were near Broadway when Shaft finally flashed on to where they were going and what he was going to do. He pulled up to a walk, noted with satisfaction that Buford was breathing harder than he was and that half-moons of sweat darkened his jacket under the arms.

'Hey, man,' he gasped. 'You got any subway tokens?'

Buford began fishing in his pocket. Shock and action had worn him down to a simple reflex without thought. Shaft smiled. Smiled in the chest-heaving, heart-pounding, brain-banging movement in the false dawn of a Harlem street light and acknowledged, to himself and for himself, his capacity to survive. Look at Buford. He talked about this but he wasn't prepared for it. He was honking so hard his hand was shaking, spilling dimes into the street. Shaft reached out, held Buford's fistful of change steady and sorted it out with a finger until he found tiny tokens hiding under pennies. There'd be no attendant at the turnstile he wanted to use.

'I'm going to take you to meet some friends of mine,' he told Buford. 'You make one fucking remark about any Tom shit to these people and I'll break both your legs.'

Then he turned and led the way toward Broadway and the Seventh Avenue IRT. He walked. It was maybe 4:45 or 5 o'clock. Anybody saw them now would figure they were just a couple of studs coming back from a party or a couple of Toms going off to sweep floors. If anybody handed him a broom right then, he thought, he'd climb up on the small end of it and sleep twenty-four hours.

Shaft's face was gentle, open, snuggled against the pillow. It was more round than oval, more flat and concave than sculptured and convex. The eyes and nose seemed to have been cut into it, rather than built upon it. It was almost a Polynesian carved face, cut into stained balsa or some dark wood. The lips were full, but they lay flat against his teeth. A mask, but not a mask. Even in sleep, there was life in it. Life and strength. It was framed in a modified Afro haircut, notched with unexpectedly delicate and tightly set ears.

The large, wide-set eyes of that face blinked open about noon. It had been an intense deep sleep, taken from the morning hours by necessity as much as desire. He felt bathed in warmth and silence, secure and safe. White people woke up with that feeling almost every day. He had known it only since the discovery of his own power and strength. He could still savor and count its worth as a grubbing trash-picker can count the treasures of unexpected discovery in the unlikely heap. Silence. He could hear Ben Buford's slow, easy breathing from the narrow rumple of sheets and pillows across the room and see almost a third of a long, angular leg protruding out from under the sheet and light blanket at the bottom of the child's bed.

Shaft got out of bed without a sound, reached for his pants hung over the back of the chair and pulled them on with the slight clink of keys and change, not enough to awaken Buford. Let the mother sleep for a while. Shaft padded out of the room on bare feet, feeling and enjoying the cleanness of the tiles. He promised himself he would clean up his apartment when he got back to it, to set up a system that would make his floors feel the same way. It was good. The chicks who got out of his bed must feel like they were walking through the Sahara with all the goddamned grit and soot that he forgot to brush away or never had time to worry about. It was nice to feel a floor like this.

The bathroom down the hall was spotless, too. He checked out the bright children's towels hanging on the racks as he stood urinating, digging the yellow plastic duck on the side of the tub. He could remember somebody soaping, rinsing and drying him off as a kid. Who the hell was that among all the people the Welfare Department had shuffled him to as a foster child? Mrs. Iggleston? Mrs. Johnson? No. He flicked the handle of the toilet. Even that was gleaming polished. Mrs. Underwood! She was the one. Nice old bitch, drank too much when the check came, but she spent at least part of it on soap and a kettle to heat the water. The rest of them? Fuck the rest of them, he thought, looking at his face in the mirror, twisting the taps together. He wanted to brush his teeth. He'd use one of the kids' half-size brushes in the rack. The kid would never know. He felt a little guilty. He also felt a twinge of concern. All the married people he knew said that the only thing you got out of the first ten years of kids was a variety of diseases they brought into the house. Which kid had the cold? Fuck it. He picked the least frazzled of the brushes, the bright red plastic one, and brushed while he traced the road-map red that patterned his eyes. Any sleep was enough sleep, but he wished he had been able to go longer. He hoped the kid didn't have anything serious. Could you catch tooth decay from somebody? No, every time he went tongue-diving with a fox it would mean . . . hell, he wouldn't have a tooth left. Fuck it. Anybody who had a house this clean wouldn't have a kid with a lot of diseases anyhow. He spat out the Crest. That was awful-tasting shit, but there was something in it that was good for you. He'd ask Helen, kind of casual, how the kids had been lately. He put the toothbrush back in the rack, sloshed water into his face from the cups of his broad, meaty hands. He would borrow Marvin's razor later.

Shaft padded out of the bathroom, poked a head into the bedroom to note that Ben was still out and snoring lightly. He pulled the door almost shut. He wasn't sure he liked Buford much anymore or that there was anything there to like or dislike. You either joined him or fought him. Who liked Lenin? Probably nobody but his mother. Shaft turned and headed toward the dish-and-water noises from the kitchen at the end of the long, carpeted hallway.

'Hey, baby,' he said to the young woman at the sink. 'You got any coffee in this joint?'

Helen Green turned, smiling. She nodded toward the stove.

'It'll be done dripping in a minute. I heard you in the bathroom. Did you get enough sleep?'

'Enough,' he said, yawning and stretching, his arms up and almost touching the ceiling of the apartment's roomy combination of a place to cook it and a place to eat it. All the muscles of his torso rippled upward and the highest of the bullet scars peeked over the top of his belt like a lost and wandering navel.

'You shouldn't do that to a grown woman this early in the day,' she said, walking over to the stove with a brown pottery mug, then juggling the hot Chemex filter in two fingers while she poured his coffee with the other hand. He broke the stretch with a laugh.

'Shit,' he said, 'all I have to do is look at you wrong and Marvin going to fix up my tax return so good I'll never see the outside of Danbury jail.'

Shaft sat on the edge of one of the tube-steel chairs, his elbows on the plastic surface of the table, counting the equipment of normalcy in the kitchen. He did it every time he came here. The bright blue canisters on the shelf beneath the cupboards, the cooking timer beside them, the glass and plastic blender plugged into the socket beside the toaster, the swing-out can opener attached to the cupboard beside the window over the sink, the chalked messages on the blackboard beside the door to the hallway. There was a place for everything in his need to see and be a part of this middle-class scene of domesticity. And everything was in its place.

'You got a new frying pan.'

'Green stamps.'

'Green stamps?'

'From the grocery store. You paste them in a little book and then turn them in for frying pans, bathroom scales and things like that.'

'Oh, yeah. That what they teach you up at Vasar?'

'What's that?' She sat down with her own cup, looking genuinely puzzled.

'They teach you how to lick all them itty-bitty little stamps and paste them in a book?'

'How would you like a hot cup of coffee over the head?'

He laughed. She picked up a pencil from the table and began to make notes on a small pad in housewife's shorthand.

Cof. Veg. Pap tls. Iv dish.

Shaft chewed on the blunt edge of the coffee mug and watched her make out the shopping list. She was the least black Negro he knew, possibly the most attractive, possibly the most feminine and womanly as well. Marvin Green was a fortunate man to have her as a wife and the mother of his children. He, John Shaft, was equally fortunate to have them both as friends and the caretakers of the one sanctuary to which he might retreat from the churning, snarling city. He couldn't really stand it for any length of time. The whole domestic scene was a huge pain in the ass, an irritant that grated against everything he felt about conformity and isolation of both spirit and flesh in the soft death of the suburbs. But he also needed occasional draughts of the warmth and viability of it, the continuing stability of its values, however boring. It was the underside of the world, the antithesis and the opposite. It had been the one place to run when there was no place else to go with Ben Buford. Helen paused in mid-vegetable, turned from the shopping list to look up at him seriously and hesitantly.

'There's been a lot of talk about it on the radio,' she said.

'Like what?'

'Five men were killed. I think they said three on the roof and two in the street.'

He had figured it would be something like that, but the vital statistics of it shook him.

'I wish it had been more,' he said.

Helen Green's eyes widened, her mouth turned down with dismay and shock. Shaft could be brutal and violent; that was his world. But he was not totally brutal and violent a person. Not to her.

'Yeah,' he said, getting up and moving toward the stove for more coffee. 'Five of their people for five of ours. Maybe something like that.'

She had turned to look at him, twisting around in the dinette chair, not quite believing that she was listening to a man in her kitchen wish for five violent deaths.

'Well, shit, Helen, if we're going to fight a revolution, if we're going to start waving guns around like that, why in the name of hell doesn't somebody learn how to use the damn things? Nowhere in the world should five men die without taking five with them if that's what it's going to be.'

'Johnny, are you all right?'

'Hell, no, I'm not all right. And neither is anything else in this fucked-up world.'

He wished he could tell her how grateful he was that there had been a place where he could run from it. From everything else in the fucked-up world, to the calm condition of her home, her kitchen. For some reason, he couldn't do that. The words stuck in his throat and even the hot strong coffee he gulped was no help in dissolving them. He was even avoiding the concerned and sympathetic hazel eyes with which she followed him across the black and white tile floor. He'd better go get Buford up. He reached for another mug out of the cupboard and poured coffee into it.

'John, who were they trying to kill? You or him?'

Shaft wished he knew. The six-and-a-half-foot egomaniac bent and folded into a five-foot child's bed down the hallway of this middle-class apartment would awaken with righteous certainty that he alone was the target, the total enemy, the lobo messiah. That was too simple. Shaft was glad she had asked; it reminded him to keep thinking while she wrapped him in the security blanket of the home.

Shaft walked back to the stove with the mugs and poured Ben Buford's coffee back into the pot. He wanted to make a couple of calls before he renewed the confrontation with Ben. Helen had put the essential question to him. Buford's answer to it wasn't going to be good enough.

'What time do the kids get home?' he asked.

'About three-thirty. They want to see you. They were tickled you and Buford were sleeping in their beds. Papa Bear and Angry Bear.'

'Hey, good! What about Marvin?'

'Maybe five-thirty. He'll call and let me know. Maybe a little earlier because you're here.'

'Tell him not to change his routine.'

She frowned again.

'Cool,' Shaft said, putting the extra cup in the sink and walking over to touch her shoulder. 'Nobody's coming in here to shoot anybody. I meant he shouldn't screw up his day. We'll be going about ten or eleven. Plenty of time to talk.'

Helen Green, who was a Negro girl two or three generations removed from the blackness of skin and soul that had brought Shaft to her kitchen in flight, raised her hand to the one on her shoulder and held it gently for a moment.

'This frightens me,' she said.

'You ain't the only one. But nobody's after you, maybe not even me. And nobody knows he's here. Relax. I got to use the telephone.'

There was an extension telephone in the kitchen. Shaft guessed it would be easier on Helen to hear little or nothing of what he had to say. He filled his mug with a third cup of coffee and started for the living room to make his calls while settled in Marvin Green's big leather chair.

'John,' she said. 'John, I . . .'

'Hmmmm?'

He paused at the entry from the kitchen into the long hallway past the bedrooms to the living room, turned and faced the questions in her eyes.

'Nothing, I guess. What do you think Ben would like for supper?'

'That mother's so mean he don't eat,' Shaft said. 'He lives on hate.'

'What about you?'

'Steak,' he said. 'Dipped in flour and fried.'

'Ugh!'

Anderozzi and the Commissioner were going back to the municipal termite nest that is the Mayor's official residence,

Gracie Mansion, when the phone buzzed in the back of the Commissioner's limousine. There had been no sleep for either of them. Anderozzi had stretched out on the leather couch in the Commissioner's office for about an hour, but they had continued to talk and consider the reports coming in from the various divisions involved in the investigation. The Commissioner insisted on dealing with the reporters personally in the sessions that followed. It was too wild for a lot of talking by uninformed deputies. Homicide said the area around 139th and Amsterdam had been cordoned off and shaken down, room by room, person by person. No witnesses to anything. Nobody knew anything. They heard some noise out there, that was all. Just some noise in the night. They thought it might have been backfire. The Commissioner had turned purple with fury.

'Five of their own people cut down with machine guns and it might have been backfire!' he shouted, wasting energy. Anderozzi kept his mouth shut.

The ballistics crew said all the slugs had been .45s and fired from any one of a variety of automatic weapons. They had a bushel basket of the ejected casings, painstakingly gathered from the street, the hallway of the building where Shaft had gone to see Buford and the rooftops of the tenements on each side. A pile of the slugs that had come from those casings had also been collected, dug from the tired walls of the buildings and from the flesh of five young men. The preliminary reports said merely that the bullets had come from the vast underground of weaponry. No one had expected them to say more. With calipers and microscopes and micrometers, the lab men would take the bullets along the path of record to the origin of the guns. Eventually. Weeks from now. It wouldn't mean much of anything when they reached the destination except to say that the guns had been lost or stolen years ago and deposited against the moment of this need. What the hell was the difference? Anderozzi thought cynically as he went through the reports. A machine gun was a machine gun, a dead man was a dead man.

The Commissioner picked up the telephone when it buzzed the rasping signal of a call. The black Mercury was turning off the East Side Drive just beyond the glimmering United Nations building and Anderozzi was letting his grainy eyes rest on the reflections swirling on the East River when the Commissioner nudged him lightly with an elbow and handed over the phone.

'It's John Shaft. Tell that sonofabitch I'm not your secretary.'

Anderozzi fought back a smile as he took the receiver and found the speak-listen control button with his thumb. The Commissioner would have misinterpreted the smile. He was weary, too. The circumstances and the city were pressing on him, but his inner smile was a signal of his own relief. As he had moved from one to another of the torn black bodies early in the torn black morning, Anderozzi had expected one of them to be John Shaft's.

'The Police Commissioner is not my secretary,' he said into the telephone. 'Uh-huh. Yes. Well, I'll tell him that. But let's talk about *you* before the FCC cancels our broadcasting license . . .'

Anderozzi glanced at the Commissioner as he listened, then back to the cool early dusk that was settling on the streets through which their driver tooled with the careless confidence of a cop, hardly stopping for the red lights, letting the official look of the car help clear the way for them.

'No,' Anderozzi said. 'We don't. Not a thing. What about you?'

The car was coming up to the mansion now, pulling into the drive to seek a place among the other black vehicles that indicated the Mayor's impatience with memos and telephones. A lot of his top people were there already.

'Where are you?' Anderozzi asked. 'I don't think it's the best idea you ever had, but I'll check.'

The car stopped. The Commissioner's glance was a signal that the conversation had to end. They had to get inside.

'No, really, nobody is after Buford that I know of.' He listened for a moment, then put the phone back with a quiet agreement. 'Okay, talk to you later.'

Anderozzi climbed out after the Commissioner.

'Shaft wants a line to the Mafia,' he said to the Commissioner's back.

'Why?'

'He isn't sure.'

'He's crazy.'

'Maybe.'

'Can you give it to him?'

'No.'

'Are you going to find somebody who can?'

'Probably.'

'The Mafia. Good Christ, what's the Mafia got to do with this?'

'Who knows . . . for sure?'

The Commissioner was about half a foot shorter than Anderozzi and had to cock his head back and peer up as he considered the question, standing on the entrance steps of the mansion.

'This is what I'm going to tell the Mayor. One. Those five men were killed by experts. How do we know? They left no clues or casualties behind. They could have been white, they could have been black. We don't know. I think the idiot is smart enough to accept that and use it to get off the hook. But if he presses the point, I'm going to tell him that everything points to

92

white. Black men don't kill that way, not when they're killing each other. I never saw a black killing that wasn't a crime of one passion or another. This wasn't. This was a goddamned massacre in the closing of a trap as only a white man would do it. Second. I'll tell him Buford was the only logical target of the assassination. Those five people were all tied to him. There was no reason to kill them except that they meant Buford. What he has then is a white attack on the most inflammatory and vital of the black militant leadership. Is he prepared for that? Is he going to tell the city that? God knows.'

The Commissioner spun around and flung himself up the steps toward the entrance, where a uniformed cop stood guard and now raised his hand in salute. Anderozzi followed, thinking about the Mafia. He remembered the confidential report that had circulated after Watts about the insurance policies on those charred slums. There was a trace of olive oil in the smoke. Nobody could tell how much. But here? What was the bridge in Shaft's mind that went from a black nationalist gun battle to the mob?

Cars were moving out of parking spaces and the underground garages of apartments at 7:35. Good, thick darkness was settling on Riverdale with the sun disappearing behind the Palisades in Jersey across the Hudson. The cars would be carrying couples down the West Side Highway, past the glimmering reflection on the river of the Palisades Amusement Park and the Crisco sign that were New Jersey's contribution to the river view. Riverdale was heading for the theater, some of it to catch a quick dinner first, but most to struggle with the hunt for a parking place. There were a lot of them making the trip. The intense young people who spoke of theater but went to musicals.

At 7:35 a black Cadillac limousine slipped into the Riverdale street of Marvin Green's apartment, found a door marked Service Entrance behind a row of shrubs and paused there with the engine breathing lightly. Two figures moved out of the confusion of landscape gardening, down the walk and folded themselves into the car's back seat. The vehicle moved away as soon as the door clicked shut and Shaft settled back against the cushions at Ben Buford's side, thinking that these big cars were as warm and soft as an unholstered pussy.

'Be a mighty surprised chauffeur if we got into the wrong car,' he said, nodding toward the dark-skinned uniformed driver who was pretending not to be checking them out in the rear-view mirror. Buford grunted. There had been little time for them to talk in the afternoon and the nationalist leader had shown no eagerness to seek conversation. He had seemed disoriented, jarred loose from the firm foundation of his ego by the echoes of the machine-gun rattles that were now vibrating through the city.

Shaft had been through with his telephone calls and was back in the kitchen, talking with Helen Green when Buford came out of the children's bedroom. Helen was just then suggesting that Shaft should get married and move to the suburbs; he had been suggesting in return that she take up sky diving as a hobby. He would if she would, he said, but they were both too young to die. She threw a potato at him, he caught it and they laughed, a spatter of chuckles that drowned in the first wave of Buford's gloomy presence.

Shaft's glance at the tall man was speculative, measuring. Helen asked, 'Did you sleep all right curled up in that bed?'

'Yes,' Buford said.

'Here, have a cup of coffee.'

'I'll get it,' Shaft said, moving to the cupboard for a cup, then to the stove. 'You want milk and sugar?'

'Yes.'

Yes, please, you sonofabitch, Shaft thought. That bastard must think the world's nothing but a bunch of white coeds, hungry for the punishment of his fire, ready to wait on him. He put the cup down at a place on the table, the coffee black.

'Milk's in the icebox,' he said. Goddamnit, pour it in your ear for all I care, he thought.

Helen said she would get it, for Ben to sit down and wake up. Buford sat. Shaft thought he looked like a big skinny bug in a museum exhibit without his jacket on and the gold-rimmed spectacles glittering a reflection of the kitchen lights. All antenna and elbows, like a praying mantis that had been trained to wear a turtleneck. Shaft's mind began to run away with the images. It wasn't his kind of thinking, but he was enjoying it, pouring out a secret or maybe not-so-secret resentment on the onetime friend of the streets. Then he pulled himself up short with a question that must have come from the last shred of his conscience, poking through to his overriding sense of reality: Why did he dislike Buford now? For going his own route? For doing more than he had done or ever considered doing about the black identity they shared?

Buford may have sensed the vulnerability of Shaft's self-examination. He chose the moment to ask, 'How many people did I lose?'

'Five,' said Shaft. The numeral scraped and grated on his throat, coming out ragged and choked. Jesus Christ, that was it. 'Dotts, Peerce and Newfield on the roof. Two downstairs.' The big hard face behind the spectacles was blank with the pain of it, then turned down to the coffee. That was it. They were Buford's people, not his. Shaft thought that if he had been anybody else but the thing he had become, he would walk across the kitchen, put his arms around Ben Buford and weep with the man for their brothers. Instead, he offered the cold half inch of reality.

'I want you to go with me this evening, Ben, to see a man who knows some answers about how and why.'

Buford nodded and was silent, as he sat silent now in the car, scanning the river and the Jersey shoreline and the liners berthed at the piers for freight or the fat cargo of spring's tourists. As he had been silent through the dinner with Marvin Green, his wife and children. As he might remain silent until he found the podium and the audience of his hatred for the voice of his violence.

Shaft lit another cigarette. He had bummed a pack of Salems from Helen. He dropped the match in an ashtray that was bigger than the radio in most cars and told Buford something of the story of Beatrice and how he was trying to find her. It was the first chance he'd had. But was Ben listening? He couldn't tell. The Cadillac suddenly, quietly, pulled up in front of Knocks Persons' castle. He wanted Buford to go in carrying the knowledge that this little bitch he'd never seen, not John Shaft, was the cause of six deaths so far. Maybe a lot more to come.

Chapter Six

'I F WE do not have the capacity to deal with these problems today and the courage for a confrontation with our mistakes of the past, then we might as well abandon this city to the chaos that will befall it. I cannot let this happen, either as your Mayor or as a citizen of a metropolis that is great in all things, even its sorrow over these tragic, shameful, wasteful deaths. Nor can you permit this to happen if you hope to live in peace, in the assurance that we are not plunging headlong toward an irretrievable condition of despair and disruption. Therefore, as your Mayor, I propose . . .'

Knocks Persons flicked a button on the television control panel. The big blue eye in the wall went dark. He touched another control and a brow of wood and matching fabric panel drooped over it, settled on bearings in the wall and hid its presence. He rubbed the ash off the even-burning end of the cigar in his left fist and raised it from the big crystal ashtray to his lips. He thought about the Mayor. What they forgot after they got there to being Mayor and things like that was where they'd come from, what the city meant and how it worked. They used to know. He remembered men who knew and made it work. They paid their dues. They used it. Some good, some bad. But they knew. This one didn't know except how to look on that box on the wall. Too many of them only knew that, nothing more. Too many of the young ones knew how to look, how to talk. But they didn't know how anything worked.

These were Knocks Persons' thoughts when the soft summons of the telephone twisted his huge body around in the vertical leather bathtub and informed him that Shaft was there with Ben Buford. Shaft. Did he know? He had to gamble that Shaft did. But there was doubt in the gamble. Maybe they hadn't let Shaft know enough as he went into their world. Maybe just enough to get by until he got himself killed. Maybe until they decided to kill him off. A touch of fear and remorse penetrated the hulk of him. Beatrice. Goddamn those motherfuckers. Let them give Shaft enough life to find her. They'd kill him sure. But let him find her first. They'd kill him sure. That was how things worked. It didn't have anything to do with the bright blue faces on the wall.

'Knocks, this is Ben Buford,' Shaft said as he came through the door at the far end of the room and waded through the pool of white carpeting.

Knocks nodded at the tall beige bag of angles and degrees. He didn't get up or offer a hand. Buford wasn't bending either. He silently assessed the big black man through the shimmering ovals of the wirebound spectacles, then granted a nod in return.

Hey, Shaft thought, these bastards really picked up on each other fast. They were so goddamn cool but their minds were tearing at each other, ripping and smashing at each other like a couple of studs hungry for the same woman. Power was the woman and they were both after her. He caught Persons' almost imperceptible gesture toward the two chairs that had been set in front of the glass desk. He also caught Buford's vibrations of hostility. Shit. They weren't going to talk to each other. Not unless he forced it. He didn't give a fuck if Persons reached right over that glass lake and pinched Buford's head off with two big fat fingers. And he didn't give a good goddamn if Buford sank his teeth into the meaty column of brown flesh that rose like a bridge abutment out of Knocks' frosty white shirt. But he wasn't going to get killed simply because he was caught between them.

'This cat knows where Beatrice is,' he said blandly, pointing a thumb at Ben, watching the bomb land on both of them, flare in the sudden ignition of shock, then blossom into a cloud of rage. He was watching it happen to Persons when Buford hit him. Stupid. He had underestimated the black nationalist. The long lean body struck him in the side of the head like a screaming spear from a catapult hidden in the forest of the white rug. A spear screaming 'You sonofabitch!' and with all the ugly thunder of Buford's anger, surprise and outrage.

The left side of Shaft's head went numb under the impact. He felt himself lifted out of the chair, spinning to the right. He tried his feet and they weren't there. They were going out sideways kicking at nothing. Shaft had a sliding, blurred image of Persons getting out of the leather bathtub with more speed than his bulk allowed. But he lost the focus in the spinning room. He had deliberately unleashed a maniac upon himself and he had about half a second to get ready for the consequences. He pulled his body together as tightly as possible and twisted to land rolling on his left shoulder. Come on, Persons, get your ass around here and grab this mad bastard.

Buford remembered the streets. He didn't stand there and weigh the damage of his blow and the satisfaction of it. He was right with Shaft all the way, on top of him, around him, the angles and points of his body flying in a quick squall of blows. Hurtling toward the carpet, Shaft thought he'd be going right through the floor under the hammering if Buford had forty or fifty more pounds of flesh to spend on his rage. He pulled up a knee to cover his groin and threw his right arm in front of his face, to push when he landed and to cover his chin and eyes. He held the left close to his side, feeling, rather than thinking that he would throw it once into the center of Buford's storm. He didn't want to hurt him, just bring him under control now. He hit the carpeting, twisted. All right, now! He swung. Nothing. The fist sliced through empty air and filled the vacuum of Buford's sudden absence.

Persons had him. That was power, Shaft thought, the big, ham-big hands, holding Buford by the arms but containing the entire writhing length of the man in a double vise. The strength of the grip went all the way down through the hard core of Persons' bulk. Shaft lay on the floor for a moment, watching Buford lash and lunge like a marionette hanging on steel strings. Buford's glasses had twisted off in the fray. He looked about five years younger and a lot dumber. A foot lashed out and caught Shaft in the hard muscle of the calf of his left leg. That sonofabitch had the longest legs in the world. He was screaming out of his mind.

'I'll kill you, you rotten faggot cocksucker,' Buford shouted.

That was the language he wanted to hear from Buford. Down to the basics. Never mind all that revolution shit. This was the only level where he would get what he wanted from Buford. Shaft started getting off the floor, careful to stay out of range of the big flying feet.

'Fuck you!' he shouted at Buford.

Persons was bellowing, too.

'Stop it, goddamnit!'

Good. Persons was mad, too. Beneath that ton of lard and muscle, there was a place where it was possible to get to Persons. Shaft let them roar. It was doing them all good. Buford was raging out of an almost catatonic blankness that had cloaked his reactions since the shooting and the flight to Marvin Green's apartment; Persons was forced to feel and react with more than his massive imperturbability, a man forced to deal with a dog fight in the middle of his carpet. And he, Shaft, was in control.

There was a moment's lull, as there is in the eye of a hurricane. A dead, dramatic calm. He used it to pull the still unopened envelope of Knocks Persons' money out of his jacket and throw it down on the glass desk. Persons and Buford were ludicrous figures, standing before him in a dance of lunge and restraint.

It was an outrageous gesture. Shaft was slightly apprehensive himself; he wondered with a twinge if he would ever get his hands on the envelope again. It depended on how they reacted next, these two angry black men who were so distinctly apart from both his own anger and his own blackness.

'I'm going to get the fuck out of here and let you two eat each other,' he snarled. 'You, you sonofabitch,' he leveled a finger at Buford, 'are the biggest goddamn phony in the world. Revolution, my ass. You just found a new way to chase pussy. How much homework you ever done? How many dues you paid? Shit, you just found something to do besides go to jail for being stupid. Four o'clock this morning, some cats came around to show you how much you didn't know.'

He had to cut deep, get to the core of Buford and split him open. He hoped Persons was hanging on.

'There'll be statues to you all over Mississippi one of these days, with big letters all over them saying, "This here is the nigger who led the sheep to slaughter."'

His eyes burned into Buford's with every word. He had not looked at Persons. Now he did, saying, in a softer, slower voice, 'And you, you're worse. He's a crazy Judas, but you got maybe a couple thousand dollars in the bank for every piece of brain and bone that's sprayed around on that roof. You got the silver. Yeah . . . you got the silver *and* . . . *you'd* . . . *lie* . . . *every goddamn* . . . *one* . . . *of* . . . *us* . . . *into* . . .

hell . . . for . . . more . . . of . . . it . . . including . . . your . . . own . . . daughter . . . including . . . every . . . black . . . man . . . in . . . the . . . world . . .'

Shaft turned and strode toward the door. He wasn't sure he could get out of the building alive. But he wasn't going to act like he couldn't. Halfway across the room, he stopped to finish it.

'You know what I mean?' he asked, turning to them, noting that Persons no longer held Buford, that they simply stood there watching him. 'I mean neither one of you bastards is worth a damn to me, to the black people, to Beatrice, wherever the hell she is right now.'

He turned and left them. There were the men outside the door. They looked at him but said nothing. Shaft walked evenly but not quickly along the gleaming oak-paneled hallway to the elevator door. The black plastic button was set in a brass plate. Or maybe it was gold. Christ, Persons could have a platinum elevator if he wanted.

One the edge of his peripheral vision, Shaft was watching the two men at the gates to Knocks' sanctuary. He pushed the black button with a fat thumb and heard the machinery of the small lift begin to whirr. He was counting. He was up to 120, 121, 122 . . . The guards at the door stiffened slightly, their slouching suits rising out of the creases of inactivity. The door opened. Shaft concentrated on the elevator button.

'Shaft,' Persons rumbled at him. He turned his grim face to the man whose bulk filled the doorway. The guards also looked to Persons, their faithful eyes wanting to know if they should run and retrieve Shaft like a stick on the beach, a ball in the field. Persons ignored them. So did Shaft. 'You want to come back and talk this out?'

Shaft looked at him with what he hoped to be disdain or at least indifference.

'What?' he pretended deafness.

'You want to come back here and talk . . . a little?'

He had the bastards. It was in the pause, in the modification of the request. He probably had Buford, too. He would have paid one hundred dollars for a transcript of the conversation that followed his departure from the room. The one hundred twenty-second exchange, spoken or shouted, in which the two of them had decided that the bullshit was over and they would now get down to it with Shaft – provided Shaft could be brought back to do it.

'Straight?' Shaft asked. The guards at the door must be wigging over the dialogue. They had probably never heard Persons involved in an equal exchange. He got reports and gave orders. Who was this cat in the rumpled gray suit, torn out at the shoulder a little, who was treating Knocks Persons like something else?

Straight, Shaft asked. Were they going to level? There was no alternative now. They had forced him into the position and had to accept it.

'Straight,' Knocks promised, reaching into a back pocket for the handkerchief about the size of a schooner sail, dabbing at the perspiration across his heavy brow.

The elevator door hissed aside. Shaft glanced from Persons to the small chamber that would carry him down to the street – and he knew now that he could make the journey without interference – and then looked back to Persons. Waiting. Let the man take one more measure of the importance of his decision.

'Straight,' he repeated, turning back toward the room, again walking evenly but not quickly.

Ben Buford had apparently picked up the chrome and leather side chairs they had knocked over in the outburst and was sitting slumped into one of them, gnawing on the knuckle of his left thumb. His right hand was resting on his thigh and the fingers diddled nervously in a rippling drumbeat of anxiety or exasperation. He didn't look up.

Shaft took the chair beside Buford. Persons immersed himself in the leather bathtub.

'What do you want?' the big man grumbled. The envelope of money still lay on the glass. It had not been moved from the spot where Shaft dropped it. The question was implicit with Persons: did he want more money?

Shaft ignored the nuance for the substance of the moment. Of course he wanted more money. He wanted money and money and money. But there was a line he had to draw for them.

'Two things,' Shaft said. 'From you, I want to know who the hell is after you and why. From him – ' he turned his head to nod at Buford – 'I want straight answers on what he's after as far as you're concerned and what he's willing to do to get it. You first. Where's your trouble?'

Persons had more guts than the rhino he resembled.

'Heroin,' he said matter-of-factly. 'Spanish Harlem. Over around One Hundred Sixteenth Street and Broadway.'

'Why there? That's all over.'

Persons seemed almost to be smiling at his ignorance.

'About seven, eight years ago, the Italians decided to let the retail business go. There was all this pot and pill shit goin' and everybody was pushin'. It was like a kid in school didn't have to go look for a pusher in the playground. He just go to his teacher and make a connection. It was all amateurs. Everybody was doin' it. Everybody was the pusher, everybody was the connection, everybody was the user.'

'What's that got to do with heroin?'

'Well, it was all confused. It got so nobody could keep track of what was going on, coming in, going out. All like that.

Everybody was carrying. So the Italians, they decided it was too much for them to keep track of. They couldn't do it.'

'Why not? They always kept track of it before.'

'That was before. They had people, lots of people, the young ones to train and move in with them. But where the young ones now? They goin' to some college, they goin' into the real-estate business, they goin' into keepin' track of the books and the figures instead of the pushers and the heads.'

Of course, Shaft thought. If a Mafia don was breaking his kid into the business today, he would break him in through the Harvard Business School rather than the college of the streets.

'Instead,' Persons went on, warming to his lecture, 'they figure they would just let the small stuff go to the Spanish coming in, the Cubans and the Puerto Ricans, and they'd just get theirs in moving it in and out of the country.'

'So what's that mean in trouble for you?'

'It means,' Buford interjected in his angry, preachy voice, 'that the Cubans and the Puerto Ricans didn't get a goddamned thing. He did!'

Buford meant Persons.

'You took over heroin in Spanish Harlem?' Shaft asked.

Persons gazed silently at them for a moment, then nodded.

'What's the difference?' Shaft persisted.

Again it was Buford who answered.

'About eight . . . ten million dollars a year the way he took it and expanded it. That's the guess. Only he can tell you for sure.'

It was funny as hell to Shaft. Only he couldn't laugh just yet. The Mafia had gotten out of the Spanish Harlem heroin trade because it was suffering a personnel shortage. They thought they were throwing a scrap to the Spics who could be controlled at the sources. But it didn't work that way. Crime and profit, basic to nature, won't tolerate the vacuum either. Persons had moved in. It was very funny. He had probably even absorbed the Spaniards without much difficulty. What the hell, half of them were black – and getting blacker through the integration of poverty and ghetto isolation. The Italians were no longer the lower class of crime, at least on that level. They were the aristocracy. He supposed Anderozzi knew all this. Why hadn't he mentioned it? Was he so busy looking for angry niggers under the bed with molotovs that he was forgetting the basics? That wasn't likely. The sonofabitch just wasn't leveling with him. His thoughts turned swiftly back to the money, the prize of this game.

'Eight to ten million,' Shaft said.

Persons may have considered trying to get away from the economics of it. But he couldn't get away from Buford.

'You don't count it that way,' Knocks said.

'The hell you don't!' Ben said, straightening up in the chair. 'You count every goddamn penny of it.'

'Hey, man,' Shaft said. 'No speeches.'

Buford twisted and looked at him for the first time since he had tried to smash Shaft's head from its moorings. The insane eyes were lighted anew with anger. But his voice was controlled and even.

'Maybe you need speeches, Shaft,' he said. 'Maybe you should listen sometime to what's happening. What that sonofabitch is saying is that he controls the source of more fucking misery for the black people of Harlem that Whitey ever dreamed of holding.'

Shaft couldn't help himself. 'What's the matter with you, fool, don't you believe in equal opportunity?'

'One day,' Buford said, 'it's going to be a crime for a sonofabitch like you to call himself black. For you, for him, for everybody else who stands *for* and *with* the corruption of the community. You're going to see the day when a black man doesn't suck the blood of his brother and give it back in junk and gin and drive his Cadillacs on the difference in the price. You're going to see . . .'

'Oh, for Christ's sake,' Shaft tried to protest. Buford rode right over it.

'Not for Christ's sake, for the brother's sake . . . if we have to destroy every motherfucker in the world like that pig over there or half-honky pimp like you who doesn't give a shit for anything but himself. I want to be there when they throw your body in the fire.'

'You'll never see it,' Shaft said.

'I'll see it! We'll all see it because the whole goddamn country will be burning down!'

'Well, good!' Shaft shouted. Buford had climbed half out of the chair to bellow at him. He was poised now in a crouch that made him seem about to leap toward the sky where he could grasp thunderbolts to hurl down at these infidels. 'Well, good! At least I know how crazy you are. Before I only suspected.'

He turned to the imperturbable mass of Knocks Persons.

'Now we both know where this is all at,' he said. 'I figured you knew all the time. I hope you know this cat wasn't talking to me. That was for you.'

'I can say for myself who I'm talking to,' Buford snapped.

'Shut up,' Shaft ordered. There was finality in it, the threat that the conversation would either go Shaft's direction or end in sudden, swift violence. Buford's mouth opened slightly, then closed. Shaft was angry. Not at Ben or anything stirred by Buford's rhetoric. He had been told all that before, one way or another. He was pissed off at himself for the time that had been wasted.

'You heard what he said,' Shaft told Persons. 'It ain't me

he's after. It's your ass or his. You smart enough to see what he's doing?'

There was no sign from Persons.

'I said he knew where Beatrice was. You knew, too, you dumb bastard.'

Chapter Seven

'You can complain to the union,' he had smartassed Persons, 'but twelve-fifty an hour is only my rate for living. I get a lot more for dying.'

Shaft went out of the brownstone lair with ten thousand dollars tucked into an inside pocket of the gray suit jacket. It was ten times more than had been in the first envelope; he had told Persons that he would expect ten thousand more when and if he could deliver. Take it or leave it. It wasn't blackmail, he thought, just a reappraisal of the job hazards on the basis of more realistic information. For now the hunt began. Now he knew what he was hunting.

Ben Buford walked out with him, seeming to burn less fiercely with the inner angers. He was like a dog, Shaft thought. It made him feel better to bark and snarl once in a while. Or even bite.

'You want to deal with that man,' Shaft told him as they walked toward the corner through the midnight mist. 'Now's your chance.'

Shaft wished he had his raincoat. He couldn't remember where it was – the office, Anderozzi's cubicle, maybe back at the apartment. At Ellie's? If anything more happened to the suit, be wouldn't be able to walk the streets in it. He dealt with a nice guy named Burke at Paul Stuart. Burke wouldn't recognize this rumpled rag bag as the child of his salesmanship. But, then, Burke probably wouldn't believe where the suit had been in the last twenty-four . . . forty-eight – no, Christ! – almost seventy-two hours since he had gotten into it. The night traffic along Broadway was heavy. Shaft tried to think why. Thursday. The stores had been open late. People stopped to complain about the prices at Bloomingdale's. The more they complained, the more they ate. Late traffic. A lot of people with headaches.

'But,' he went on when Buford remained silent, 'you can't kill him. You give some and take some. That's the way he lives.'

Buford glanced up and down the divided avenue and its collection of small, dark shops. He had made two calls from Persons' coin telephone in the closet. More men would be coming to him from the replacement depot of his underground army.

'It's not the way we live anymore,' Buford said without the emphasis of contention, just stating it.

'Look, man.' Shaft sighed. 'I don't want to get into this with you again. Not now. Maybe sometime. But not now. I got a job to do and I'm going to do it. That job is to get that man's daughter back. I don't and I *can't* give a shit if he sells slaves to George Wallace. I'm still going to do it, one way or another.'

He raised his arm at the advancing rooflight of a cab. The turn indicator on the yellow Chevy blinked and the driver pulled over to collect him. A black driver. Sometimes life was so simple.

'I'm going to call you if I need you,' Shaft said, reaching for the handle.

'What if that was the CIA last night and not who you think it was?'

'You talk any Spanish?'

'A little, why?'

'You better go hide your ass in Cuba if it's who *you* think it was.'

110

He got in and began to pull the door shut.

'Ben,' he finished with him, 'I'm sorry you lost those cats.' He jerked the door shut before Buford could reply, if, indeed, there would have been a reply.

'The Village,' Shaft told the driver, who had screwed his head around on rolls of fat and was peering at him under the bill of a plaid cap. 'Just go down Ninth Avenue. Past Fourteenth.'

Why, he thought, the dirty bastards had been trying to kill *him* just because Knocks Persons had come down to Times Square with his problem and dumped it on Shaft's desk. His mind went weaving through the results and the twists of what had happened like a little old lady doing a broken-field run through the tightly packed outdoor vegetable stands the cab was passing along Ninth Avenue, some of them still lighted and doing business. He marveled with a shake of his head and a wry smile into the darkness at how quickly and coolly they had set up the hit. He had been so convenient for them. They must have been watching every move Persons made since they snatched Beatrice. Knocking off his first contact would have shown Persons how helpless he was, surrounded, alone. And it could have come off as just another race thing. Shaft was certain the police thought that's what it was, anyhow. He was certain they *wanted* to think that, rather than pry up the lid on the sewer that ran even lower than the one through which they had to swim each day. What if Buford's people hadn't been standing in the doorways with machine guns under their raincoats?

Screw what-if questions, he told himself. It's strictly what *is* in this goddamned world. You better know it. The world took what-if questions apart and made you eat them. The cab went past Twenty-second. Ellie's street. He hadn't even called her. She would be going to bed now. He wanted to tell the silent, hunched driver to swing down the block and let him off so he could crawl between the soft, smooth sheets with her, let her smooth, soft legs intertwine with his as they curled together to sleep. For all he knew, the bastards were sitting outside her apartment now, waiting to take off the top of his head with a shotgun. Shit! Why did he torture himself this way? His life was on the line and he was thinking about some fox. It didn't matter what he wanted at the moment. The job was finding out what they wanted in exchange for Beatrice. There was a progressive scale of greed to the rackets. Maybe, like Ben Buford, they wanted all of Persons. White or black, somebody always had.

When the cab ran out of Ninth Avenue and it became Hudson Street, the driver announced, 'Here's Fourteenth.'

'Just keep going. Three or four more blocks.'

The meat-packing warehouses were dull globs of inactivity in the night. In a few hours, they'd light up and bring the West Village to life, getting the stiff, fatcaked carcasses off the hooks and out to the butchers and big restaurants. This part of the Village was like a suburb of the bag of worms squirming over where Bleecker ran into Sixth and went on to Sullivan, MacDougal, Thompson and the bullshit carnival. It was close enough but quiet enough. Now it might be too quiet.

'The street after the next light,' he said. 'Jane Street. Turn there. I'll get off on the corner of the next block.'

Jane Street. He glanced at his apartment building on the corner, a white-painted, four-story brick building that went two apartments deep into Jane, toward Eighth Avenue, but halfway down the block of Hudson Street. His eyes went automatically to the windows of his own apartment in the third-floor corner. Had he left the blinds closed? They were closed now. He usually did that. But sometimes he didn't. He liked to walk around without clothes, getting coffee, ducking into the shower, shaving, getting another cup of coffee. But it had been so long since he'd been there. He occasionally flicked the blinds open before he left so he wouldn't be coming back to a dark, gloomy cave. But he couldn't remember.

The driver made the right on Jane Street, around the entrance to the Cézanne apartments, one of the big, red-brick clusters where girls with roommates, fags with roommates, young couples with dogs as roommates find refuge – with laundry facilities in the basement. The orange globes around the entrance to the No Name Bar opposite his building leered at the street like jack-o'lantern teeth. They might be sitting in there watching his apartment, waiting for the light to go on. He hoped so. There were so many freaks in that joint they'd drive a couple of ordinary, half-sane assassins right up the wall. The music pounding at them, the drunken broads babbling at them, the bummy writers insisting on telling them what they almost wrote that day and might try tomorrow.

Shaft tipped a quarter on the dollar forty-five fare and stepped into the cool, wet air of the night. It was nearly one o'clock. He shrugged against the slight chill that penetrated the suit. Spring pissed around forever getting to New York. Then suddenly it was summer. The long, hot summer. He thought he would get an air conditioner this year. Knocks Persons would buy him a piece of cool. He glanced up and down Jane Street. The Volkswagens were snugged in nose to tail with the Triumphs and Fiats – long rows of oddly shaped dogs exchanging introductions.

To the best of his eyes, there was nobody around or near the entrance to his place. But who was sitting in the cars? Or leaning in an entryway? Or up there behind the venetian blinds in his apartment? He stood at the side door of the No Name for a few moments, thinking of the odds for and against them wanting to take him here. The nice thing about dealing

113

with pure bastards, he thought, is they didn't waste a lot of time getting between points. They wanted him dead, they'd get him dead, but they would do it at a time and place that was most efficient and least troublemaking for them. It might seem circuitous or illogical to others, but to them it would be direct.

Nothing to it, Shaft, he told himself, *all you got to do is put yourself in some crazy guinea's head, walk around the scorched hills of Sicily for a hundred years on your way to Spanish Harlem and figure out how and why you want to kill John Shaft, a previously unheard-of spade who's screwing around with the nice orderly process of organized crime. Then,* he let the thought ramble, *you come back into the head of John Shaft and figure out how you get to them before they get to you.*

'Balls,' he muttered, moving to go into the No Name, opening the side door a slice to let the blast of words and warmth riding over the jukebox rock splash against his face with surf smells of alcohol and bodies. He hoped a couple of them would be sitting at the far corner of the bar, watching his apartment. It would make it so much simpler to get in touch with them.

They were there, all right. Two of them. Shaft's blackness against a white world was less contrast than their dark evil against the light mood of the drinkers, even the arguers. These had to be the bottom of the barrel, he thought. You figured if those bastards were going to have somebody hit, they sent to Detroit or St. Louis for a couple of salesmen-looking executioners who got into your life, did the job of closing it, and then got out as smoothly as precision parts in the great low-tolerance machine. He acknowledged that this was another cliché, that the two men at the front of the bar could survive as clichés in a society with great traditions of violence and that he might die of its overworked application.

The bar in the No Name runs about thirty feet from back to front, makes a slight elbow to the right and ends there against a dark, oak-paneled wall, about four feet from the window. They had the end seats, looking out into Hudson Street, up onto the windows of Shaft's kitchen, living room and bedroom on the third floor. The fire escape went right past the living-room window. The front door to the building was in clear view just around the corner, on Jane Street. That was the advantage for people like this. Architects designed the world so killers could sit like fat toads waiting for the next meal to fly by. Zap! the sticky tongue shot out. Blip! the meal was over.

Shaft thought they looked like toads, too. But he wasn't a mosquito straying out of formation. He started to slip off his suit jacket as he moved into the crowd. They were about thirty or thirty-five, he thought. Old enough to know the business, tough enough to have survived in it, dumb enough to still be taking orders for things like this. He jostled against a threesome of two fat girls oozing out of miniskirts and a seedy young guy in tweeds. Everybody in the West Village looked like a writer. Few of them ever wrote anything except bad checks. But fat girls never complained about bad checks from seedy-looking writers.

There were four big black men bunched around a small blond chick at the near end of the bar where the drop-leaf panel lifted and gave the bartender a way to get in and out. Whoever it was, he had to come around about three times on the average No Name night and throw somebody into Hudson Street, that somebody protesting that he'd never be back to drink in that lousy goddamn joint again – until tomorrow. The black cats would never make out, Shaft thought, as willing as the chick probably was. They still needed the security of numbers in the great pussy hunt when it was the lonely stalker who invariably found the game.

Rollie Nickerson, a tall skinny actor who was usually stoned out of his skull, was working behind the bar, the long spidery arms, shooting out like exploding pistons to grab a bottle, swipe the bar, plunge a glass and scoop up ice. Probably on speed. The amphetamines hammering energy out of him and burning up his brain cells. The bartenders at the No Name were either frantically busy or just standing there stoned, smiling into the pleading eyes of the customers. Nobody complained. If it got too bad, they just went up Jane Street to the Bistro or down Hudson to the White Horse. It was part of the circuit. A man was entitled to get stoned.

Shaft pushed against the crowd, rolling up his sleeves over the heavily veined and muscular forearms. His inspection bounced back and forth from Nickerson to the two men at the end of the bar. And everybody else in the joint. There were people there who knew him well enough to call his name, to turn to the men and say, 'There's Shaft. The guy you've been . . .'

But those two couldn't be dumb enough to tie themselves to the name of a man they planned to knock off. He had to play it strong, anyhow. He got the envelope of cash out of the jacket pocket, opened it close to his face like a poker player trying to squeeze aces out of a queen's ear. The bills were so damned big. He had to hunt for the fifties, finally found a couple and palmed them out of the envelope before stuffing the package into his left rear pants pocket.

He pushed into the cluster of black cats surrounding the giggling white chick. He recognized at least one of them as being from the neighborhood. The others were strangers and they frowned with hostility on his intrusion. There may be security and confidence in numbers, but who was this sonofabitch come to play in their game?

'It's cool,' he said to the one he recognized, probably a super from one of the big buildings somewhere around there. Shaft handed him his coat, the tie now pushed into a side pocket. 'Hold this a minute, will you?'

The man was smashed enough to take the coat without making a big thing out of it. He wore a beret pulled down over his right ear.

'Who you gonna fight?' he asked.

'Got to get to work,' Shaft said, moving toward the panel that led behind the bar. The others relaxed. Shit, the man wasn't after the woman. He just had to work. They smiled. 'I'll take it from you when I clean up a place to put it.'

'It look like a good coat,' the drunk said. 'If I get three or four dollars for it, I may not be here.'

The others laughed. So did Shaft. He didn't feel it, but he laughed, still keeping track of Rollie Nickerson and the far end of the bar.

'That's all good,' he said. 'But when you get to the cat I stole it from, don't ask more than four.'

Everybody except the blond chick thought it was funny. She seemed threatened by his confidence, glibness. She kept her pink nose in some gin drink she was sucking on. The black men around her stood aside as Shaft moved to the small panel, lifted it, and stepped behind the bar. Now all he needed was for some fool to shout, 'Hey, Shaft, you the new bartender? How about a drink?'

But they were pretty cool, drunk or stoned. So was Rollie Nickerson. Shaft was counting on the cool with his life. Nickerson was bending over the tub of ice cubes beneath the bar and caught the intrusion with the corner of an eye. He looked up puzzled, the back of his head to the men at the end of the bar, and, recognizing Shaft, smiled. Shaft nodded. The men at the end of the bar hardly noticed. Shaft was just another spade who had come out of a cluster of spades. Just another bartender. They didn't tap him for *the* spade. He had business there or he wouldn't be there. Their man didn't.

Shaft started straightening bottles at the end of the bar, asked the group of black men and the blond chick if they wanted another drink.

'You buy a round, I'll give you back your coat.'

'Sure. What you drinking?'

Nickerson was coming his way now, but still cool. Shaft turned and extended his hand in greeting. Nickerson went along with that. His expression changed when the two fifties found a new home. He glanced down, saw the numerals at the corner of the green wad and moved the message casually on to his pocket.

'Why don't you go around the other side and have a drink?' Shaft said.

'You just bought yourself a saloon,' Nickerson agreed, giving him a familiar slap on the shoulder as he began to move past Shaft to the exit. He should give a shit. For one hundred dollars he could get a cut-rate dentist to start capping his teeth. With a mouthful of glittery, Christ, he could be a star. The owner didn't come around until three or four to count the money and lock up. All he had to do was back Shaft's play, whatever it was.

'Where's the heat?' Shaft asked.

Nickerson paused. A few months earlier – at the height of the Christmas saloon robbery season – he had shown Shaft the snub-nosed .38 Colt that hung by its trigger guard on a small hook screwed into the underside of the bar. He had even asked Shaft, as a detective, what he should do if and when it came time for some random hood to knock off the register.

'Forget you got it,' Shaft said. 'Be nice, smile, give the man all the money.'

He had pushed it back across the bar and Nickerson had returned it to the hook, gingerly and respectfully.

'Same place,' he said now. 'I never touch the stuff.'

Nickerson went on around the corner, into the small noisy clusters. Shaft went to work. He bought a drink for the four black men and the blond chick. She was drinking vodka, not gin. All the blonds were drinking vodka this year, he thought. He poured about three shots into her highball glass and a dollop of tonic water. Somebody was going to carry her home. He didn't care who. He spent more time than he should with them. He wanted the men at the end of the bar to notice him, to identify him with the blacks. It was the best and oldest black camouflage. They all looked alike. The gunmen were looking for one who looked different and would show himself by turning up at the apartment across the street.

Shaft checked them out whenever his head was turned in that direction, on the way to the ice cubes, the register. They were sitting, smoking, occasionally touching the glasses in front of them, but barely drinking. They apparently accepted the change in shifts and the new bartender as a matter of course. They were unfamiliar with the bar's operation. So was Shaft. He hadn't spent that much time there. The register, the goddamned register. It was a complex, curious collection of keys. He remembered quickly that the black bar down the side was the one the bartender hit with the heel of his hand after punching out the price of the drinks. He hit it and the drawer sprang open. Leave the motherfucker open, he told himself.

'Give us a couple of beers, will ya?'

He gave the voice a couple of beers. He was falling into the rhythm of the work. Goddamn, look at those mugs of beer. Perfect. It made him thirsty for a glass of beer, until he remembered that he didn't like beer. He was thirsty for the perfection of drawing it. He grabbed a mug from the cluster of them beneath the bar and drew one. Perfect. Then he didn't know what to do with it. He looked up for a beer drinker, put the mug in front of him and said, 'Have one on the house.'

There was a sense of completion in the act of selling a commodity for which the demand seemed endless. That's why bartenders always looked so happy. For all of the pains in the ass that alcohol inspired, the man who served it was always in demand. He identified with the product. Shaft got a small chaser glass off the drying towels, hunted up the quart of Johnnie Walker Black Label on the high shelf in front of the mirror. He poured an inch of amber into it, raised it and let the golden heat roll down his throat. A toast to nobody, a toast to himself.

He was beginning to sweat lightly and that felt good, too. The phone rang. It startled him, coming so clearly through the noise of the jukebox and the drinkers. The phone was set under the bar, down at the end where the hoods were sitting. He finished squeezing a lime into the quinine water for a tired gin drinker and went down to it. The two men looked up at him. Shaft pointed at their glasses.

'You ready?'

'Not yet,' the older one said.

Shaft reached the phone out of its nook with one hand and held it to his ear. He smiled at the men. They smiled back at him.

'No Name,' he said.

'Is Alex Palmer there?' a querulous, unhappy voice asked. How did anybody in that condition dial a telephone?

He held the mouthpiece away from his lips.

'Either one of you guys named Alex Palmer?' he asked. Their faces were blank and they shook their heads. Shaft turned away from them and pretended to scan the room.

'Not here,' he said into the phone.

'Look, if she comes in will you tell her to call . . .'

The name was a mumble.

'Sure,' Shaft said. 'I'll tell her.'

He hung up. He enjoyed the feeling of standing close to the men. How does a tiger in the bush feel when the hunter stands two feet away, lighting a cigarette, studying the tracks? A little excited? A little nervous? Or confident, in control. He felt confident, in control. If they knew who he was, they were as cool as he was. They had a system and they didn't vary it. One of them was always looking out the window, seemingly casual and bored. When he turned back to the bar, the other was automatically turning to look out and maintain the unbroken vigil. They didn't speak to each other much. Or monosyllables that he couldn't catch.

He caught up with the demand at the bar, noticed that the crowd was thinning out. They were all really nine-to-fivers at heart. It was almost two o'clock and they had to get up in the morning, put on their straight office clothes and go to work. It was bad enough just being alive. They couldn't get bombed every night to boot, although a lot of them tried. The phone. The wonderful phone.

He went back to the end of the bar.

'Ready yet?' he asked them.

'Sure,' said the one in a hound's-tooth sport jacket over a red polo shirt. 'Club and water. Both of them.'

The other one looked like a businessman, Shaft thought as he got the bottle of Canadian Club and poured out the shots. He wore a dark sharkskin suit with a white shirt and a narrowish tie with a small pattern. Just a couple of guys having a couple of drinks. He dropped fresh ice cubes into their glasses, tipped the shots in after them and added water from a small pitcher. He suddenly remembered that he didn't know how much they had been paying a shot for the drinks. He could fake it with the rest of the customers. But not with these two.

'The house buys one,' Shaft said, getting another chaser glass and the Johnnie Walker bottle. He poured an inch and a half in the glass and raised it in a toast. Drink with me, you motherfuckers, his mind roared. They raised their glasses in a toast and sipped with him.

'Thanks,' said the sports coat.

'Sure,' said Shaft. 'Happy days.'

The liquor felt warm, strong and positive as it drifted into his stomach. They didn't know who he was and they were beginning to love him. Shaft smiled. They smiled. He bent down under the bar and reached for the telephone. There was the .38 dangling in a dull blue-black gleam like the head of a snake from a vine. It was as warming and confidence-giving as the Scotch. He smiled at the gun. He could swear the muzzle smiled back.

Shaft made one more circuit of the bar. Rollie Nickerson came giggling away from one of the tables along the wall where he had found a couple of girls without men.

'Three vodka and tonic, my good man,' he ordered.

'Your ass,' Shaft said. 'I'm your worst man.'

'Hey, you ever hear that Jelly Roll Morton stuff where he tells Lomax how the old studs used to put each other down?'

'I got those records, man,' Shaft said, pouring vodka into the three glasses, splashing tonic down on them and hunting around for a lime.

Sure he had those records. Anybody who knew anything about music and black men had them. Jelly Roll sitting there at the piano telling Lomax what it was like in New Orleans and all the other places. Jelly's foot tapping, his voice grinding gravel for the tape. Nickerson meant the scene where Jelly tells how a confrontation was built on a crescendo of threats and outrageous warnings. It was funky, old-fashioned nigger talk that Lomax made part of history by recording for the Library of Congress. Shaft cried when he read Lomax's book years ago. Somebody at NYU turned him on to it. He laughed when he heard the records. Jelly Roll, so fucking proud and beautiful. Finally stabbed to death in a Washington, D.C., bar by some other cat. Argument over a woman. That was a good way for Jelly Roll to die. The only way. He got the bottle of Johnnie Walker and poured himself another drink and poured a shot of straight vodka for Nickerson.

'Jelly Roll,' Shaft toasted.

'Jelly Roll,' Nickerson chimed, looking glazed and vague. He put the empty glass back down on the bar. 'How long you want to stay back there?'

'I don't know,' Shaft said. 'I may never leave.'

'Good. You want me to pay for my drinks?'

'Fuck it.'

'You're a good bartender.'

Shaft could feel the liquor as he watched Nickerson take the three vodka tonics back to the little table. The chicks looked pretty good to him. A little chewed up around the edges, but young, real and what the hell did he expect to find sitting around the No Name at two o'clock in the morning? *Vogue* models? Or chicks like this, or the blond down there with her pack of hounds in pursuit? Better these than the tight-ass chicks he ran into all day. He was part of their fantasies. Scared hell out of them. Big black man with his big black . . . They all ran home to the mother of a warm, oily bath, to stretch out in the suds and play with themselves while they thought about it. It was better that way. If they tried it, that would spoil everything. It would turn out to be just another piece of ass. The fantasy was much more fun than the fact. He poured himself another shot of Scotch, a little bigger than the others, raised it in a toast to tight-ass chicks and let it funnel down his throat. Women.

He turned and worked his way back up the bar, emptying

ashtrays, swiping up the water circles and whisky spills with a damp cloth.

'How you doin'?' he asked them. They were dark, heavy men, beyond the age of the racket beginners who usually got such jobs as this to prove themselves. They were professionals, he thought.

'Just fine,' one of them said.

'Have another drink,' Shaft insisted, setting up two extra glasses. They had barely touched the last ones.

They smiled at his generosity.

'Easy,' the checked sports coat said. 'Got to go easy. Got to drive home.'

But he said it jovially, fraternally. This was a good spade. You wouldn't see this one out starting riots, mugging people, slashing the canvas on your uncle's new Cadillac convertible. This one bought drinks.

'Can't drive on one wheel,' Shaft said. He put a glass on the bar for himself and got the Scotch bottle with the Canadian Club. His words sounded hollow in his own ears. Everybody's words sounded hollow. They were all drunk, he thought. He continued to think about women.

He got the phone out from under the bar and dialed. Then he pushed the disconnect plunger down with a thumb. Wrong number. What the hell was it? He laughed trying to remember. He was getting loaded. He remembered.

'Yes,' she said, a voice drenched in sleep, heavy with the warmth of a lost consciousness.

'It's me.'

'John? Where are you?'

'Downtown,' he said, slipping his hand over the mouthpiece and remarking to the two hoods. 'Got to check in with these women. They get on your ass, man, you got trouble.' The hoods smiled and nodded. They understood. They knew all about black men and black women. They finished their drinks in appreciation of Shaft's predicament with his black woman.

'Are you coming here?' Ellie asked. 'What time is it? Oh, God, it's nearly two.' She found the illuminated clock beside the bed. Shaft envisioned her reaching out from a burial mound of sheets and blankets to grope for it with one long, slender arm, white against the night. He wanted to feel the sweet touch of the hand. 'Darling, what is it?'

'Just checking in like you said I should. I'm going to be tied up with these people for a few hours.'

'John, you sound like you've been drinking. Are you drunk?'

'Hey!' He winked at the men. 'I had a couple. I ain't drunk. Just talking business with these people. Just going to be a couple hours late is all.'

'Darling, I don't understand. I'm going back to sleep Ring the bell hard and I'll get up and let you in.' She hung up.

'I'll 'splain it all when I get there,' he said into the dead phone. Jesus, but he almost said 'gits dere.' 'All right, baby, you jus' get some sleep. Don't you worry. No. Now you know I ain't doin' nothing. Don't be sitting around there worrying yourself. Jus' go to bed and get some sleep. Okay. Okay.'

He looked a little crestfallen as he put the receiver in the hook.

'Sheeyut,' he said. 'Women jus' don't give a man no room at all to play.' He reached for the Scotch bottle again as they smiled in oily understanding.

'Gives you hard time?' the one in the business suit asked.

'Not as hard as I give her.'

They laughed at that. They were still laughing when he dialed another number and let it demand another presence from the night of sleep. He reached for the Scotch with his free hand and sipped at it.

'Anderozzi,' the voice said. Sleepy, too, but hard and ready.

'Hey, baby,' Shaft chuckled as lasciviously as he could. 'How you doin'?'

'Who is this?'

'Hey, baby. This is Jelly Roll. I been thinkin' 'bout you.'

How quickly would Anderozzi pick up on the voice? Goddamnit, wake up!

'Yeah, well, I been thinkin' 'bout you, too, Shaft. But right now I'm sleeping. What the hell do you want?'

'How 'bout you comin' down to see old Big Jim? I got what you want, baby.'

The two men were fascinated. They were forgetting their routine of watching out the window. Listen to this black stud make out with that broad. Listen to him sweet talk her into the compliance that was so sweet and easy for her. They knew all about black men and black women.

Anderozzi was totally awake.

'Okay,' he snapped. 'Where are you?'

'Look, honey. I'm down to the No Name Bar right now, but this old bar got to close some time. They gonna throw old Jim out in the cold. How 'bout you comin' down here?'

'How many are there?'

'Oh, it's 'bout two right now. Yeah.'

'Where?'

'Up front, baby. I'm up front with you.'

The two hoods were excited. They weren't sure how he was going to make out. They looked eager, warm about it. They wanted him to get the girl in the end.

'We'll come in on all sides of the place. For Christ's sake, get down on the floor. Don't play hero.'

'Hey, baby,' he murmured. 'Now that's the sweet talk I likes to hear. Don't you worry 'bout the cab. Old Big Jim gonna take care of that.' He raised his eyes to the leering hoods. 'And you, too.'

Give or take a few degrees of tension, he thought it was his coolest moment. He wondered who else he might call as he put down the receiver and shared smiles of male duplicity with the hoods. He discarded the idea of another call. Too foolish.

'Coming across?' one of them asked.

'Yeah, man,' he cackled.

He shook the idea of playing games out of his head. That was the whisky talking; he wasn't drunk enough or fool enough to be listening. He leaned back against the wood of the back bar, raised one foot up on the low shelf that ran under the bar itself. Nickerson or somebody else had left a package of Marlboros on the shelf. Shaft shook one out of the box, lighted it and blew smoke out his nostrils like a black dragon. In about ten minutes, give or take an eternity, those clowns were going to look up and see a green and white patrol car drive through the front door of the No Name Bar. Maybe the side door at the same time.

He leaned down to look once again at the pistol hanging under the mahogany.

'Almost out of lemons,' he said when he straightened up. One of the men glanced at him quizzically. 'Use a lot of lemons here,' Shaft added. 'Maybe three, four dozen a . . .'

He had the gun in his hand as soon as he saw what was happening. It was one second before the hoods reacted. The three figures came in the side door. They said nothing. They stood in line with 12-gauge Remington shotguns leveled at the faces of the men at the bar, over and around the few customers who remained.

In that second, Shaft's hand came up and rested on the bar, the muzzle of the pistol about fifteen inches from either of the two. Two figures glided past the window a few feet away and pushed into the No Name through the front door. Two more shotguns.

'No, no,' Shaft said coldly and clearly. 'Just don't do it. Just sit there.'

They were stunned. Awareness lighted in their eyes. They were trained and practiced at this. They could smell a cop around a corner and down a city block. Now they had five of them around them, moving around them in a circle of riot guns and a big black man at their backs with a cocked pistol.

'Up!' he said when they checked the automatic movement toward their own guns. 'Up!' The manicured hands rose above their heads.

One of the cops came forward carefully, quickly, the riot gun still straight out in one hand, still at the middles of the pair. His free hand snaked with professional skill inside the jackets and waistbands and down the pants legs, coming out with three pistols that went into the capacious pockets of his black London Fog raincoat. He handed the riot gun to another one and snapped chrome handcuffs on the hoods.

'All right,' said the cop who seemed to be in charge of the detail, 'let's get 'em out of here.'

Shaft noticed that the No Name was totally silent, probably for the first time in its history.

'You coming along with us, Mr. Shaft?' the officer asked.

The two hoods turned their outrage on him. Shaft lifted the bottle of Johnnie Walker.

'You want one more before you go?' he invited.

The toad in the sports jacket spit in his face. He had only half recoiled, licking his lips, when the bottle broke across his cheekbone in a spray of whisky, glass and blood. A cop cursed. A girl screamed.

'Okay,' the head cop said. 'We'll stop at St. Vincent's first and get him sewn up. Let's go.'

Chapter Eight

H E COULDN'T help it. That's the way he was. Circumstance
and response. Cause and effect were almost like Siamese
twins of his nature, closer together than a couple of Harlem
tenements. There was no room there for thought, reflection
or perspective. The ball of his anger bounced from one hard
wall to the other before there was time. Later, it made him
wonder if he had not made a mistake. But it would be *much*
later, *months* later. And there would be no guilt or self-doubt
with his questions, for he was not questioning himself or his
actions. Only the results . . .

There was a small cut on Shaft's hand. A jagged chunk of
the Scotch bottle had tripped over the flesh of his callused palm
on its flight to the floor. The incision was neat, painless, but
bloody. Like most, he ignored the rules of antisepsis and put
his mouth over the cut to suck on it. The blood was warm,
salty and Scotch-tasting. He spat it out into the drain sink
beneath the bar.

'My name ees Count Dracula,' Rollie Nickerson said,
bugging his eyes in his Bela Lugosi imitation. 'I leev een
a kestle een Transylvania and I don't take sheet from
nobody.'

Nickerson and the girls were all that remained of the No
Name's business. The police had suggested that everybody go
home for the night. Everybody had taken it to heart. They left

Nickerson and his companions because the actor had explained that *he* was the bartender.

'That man is an imposter,' he said of Shaft, 'and these,' with a wave at the girls, 'are the night porters.'

He was smashed. The cops went away after Shaft told the officer in charge of the detail that he would talk with Anderozzi about the two hoods. There was time. He had to do something about getting himself together first. Where the hell was his coat? Hanging on a hook near the cigarette machine. He held the bleeding hand under the faucet, looking up over the rim of the bar at Nickerson and the girls. When actors got nervous, he thought, they could slip into other roles, outside the ones in which life had trapped them. Nickerson was deep into the Dracula fantasy. The girls were giggling.

'Eeef you will just let me fasten these electrodes to your loffly head, my dear,' he was saying, 'I am sure the experience will geev you a charge . . .'

Shaft considered the cut. It had pretty much stopped bleeding. There was a small tin box of Band-Aids next to the cash register. Bartenders are always slicing fingers with the lemons. One of those would be enough. The hood who had taken the bottle in the head was probably undergoing his own first aid at that moment. A lot more than this, he thought, pleased. He had felt bone give under the impact of the bottle. He checked around the bar for vodka, found a bottle of Gilbey's behind him and held it in his left hand while he pulled the cork with his teeth. The alcohol burned fiercely as he poured it into the cut. His only indication of it was the momentary bulge of muscle in his cheeks.

'As long as you are wasting good whisky, old fellow,' Nickerson said, switching off Lugosi to something like Terry-Thomas or Peter Sellers and losing the character in the fog of alcohol, 'would you be kind enough to waste a bit on us.'

Rollie pushed the glasses forward across the bar. Shaft put the vodka bottle beside them.

'Just help yourself,' Shaft said, turning to the Band-Aid box beside the register. He tore the wax paper off one of the adhesive strips with his teeth.

'Let me do it for you,' one of the girls volunteered. She was small, slender, dark and her nose was a little too big. A spinner. Was it Nickerson who had told him about spinners?

'You put them out on the end of your cock and give them a twist. They spin like the propellor on a beanie.'

Nickerson. Somebody. Whoever. It didn't matter. She wasn't bad. Her nose would go away if he looked at it long enough. It was like saying a word over and over in your head. After a while, it just didn't mean anything. Shaft handed her the Band-Aid. The lights around them went from a soft amber glow to a dim, murky shadow-outlined gloom.

She protested: 'I can't see to put on his bandage.'

Nickerson was at the small, black switchbox on the rear wall along the hall to the toilets.

'Feel your way around,' Rollie said. 'He likes that.'

She managed. Even in the darkness, the 'flesh-toned' strip of adhesive glowed against the heel of his hand where it covered the cut. The spinner's fingers against his palm were cool, quick, efficient. He wondered, remembering the line from Lenny Bruce or Dick Gregory, if Johnson & Johnson would one day bring out black Band-Aids, for the twenty-five million other flesh tones. He answered his own speculation: no, they wouldn't.

The other one, she was even a little smaller and more finely drawn than his nurse, who had gone to work pouring vodka. Nickerson came back from the lightbox.

'It should keep them out,' he said.

'Why'd you hit the man with the bottle?' the second spinner said.

Shaft was searching for another Johnnie Walker.

'He wouldn't stop putting ice cubes in the ashtrays,' Nickerson said.

'I didn't mind that so much,' Shaft said, finding the new bottle, pouring his own drink. 'But when he said our people couldn't swim there . . .'

The girl shut up about it.

'You going to close down?' he asked Nickerson.

'I have to wait until he gets here and counts the money. You?'

Shaft tilted the glass. He was only about three or four away from being stoned himself.

'I still got some work to do.' He looked at the first spinner's nose. 'Maybe change the bandage.'

He walked back down to the end of the bar, reached under it and got the .38 again. He stuck it into his right rear pocket.

'Will he notice that's gone?' he asked Nickerson.

'I don't know. Maybe.'

'Tell him the police took it with the two hoods and said they'd bring it back if they found it was registered.'

Nickerson nodded.

'You want to come help me change the bandage?' he asked the girl. Her nose looked better all the time. She picked up the cigarettes on the bar, stuck them in her purse and had one last strong pull at the vodka-tonic. She was standing beside the bar stool, waiting to go across the street with him by the time he got his coat off the wall hook.

'Take care, man,' Nickerson said.

'You, too.' He raised his hand in a small, cool wave. The .38 felt like a sash weight that would drag his pants down around his ankles. The ten-thousand-dollar package, less two fifties, bulged uncomfortably in the other pocket. He pushed open the door, then turned back as the girl went out into the night before him, 'I owe you a good one,' he said.

It was the closest Shaft could get to gratitude without embarrassing either one of them. Nickerson smiled at him and nodded at the departing, waggling behind of the girl. Shaft followed the path of the actor's eyes. It was too bad about her nose, he thought; she had a great ass.

'Wait, baby,' he said, thinking also that he didn't even know her name. 'It's the other way. That white building across the street . . .'

'Why don't you bring him in for questioning?' the Commissioner suggested.

'No,' said Anderozzi. 'He's doing better this way. Whatever he's doing.'

'Look, the Mayor isn't crazy. You want me to tell him that the Police Department of the City of New York is waiting for information and advice from some spade private eye he never heard of.'

'Then don't tell him. Does he tell you when he rides his bicycle?'

'There's no comparison.'

'There's none between what we can find out and what Shaft has been finding out, either. You know any black radicals? I don't. Shaft's talking with them. You know anybody who can deal with Knocks Persons? I don't. Shaft's working for the old bastard. You know why the Mob decides to gun down five black militants in the streets of Harlem? I don't. But Shaft sends us two greaseball punks – one with a slightly broken head – who probably know the answer, may even have been there. Forty-eight hours ago you were worried about sending tanks up Amsterdam Avenue. Now you're suggesting that I stop the man who's got his foot on the fuse.'

'I don't like the way this is going.'

'No cop could. But let's be pragmatic about it. The choice is going by the book, by the rules, making the Mayor happy, and maybe ending up with a couple hundred people dead and thirty or forty million dollars worth of riot damage, or letting one man work outside the rules and maybe preventing all that.'

'We can't protect him.'

'The hell we can't! We have to. If Shaft turns the wrong corner and plays tag with the front end of a truck, we've had it.'

'How tough is he?'

'Not as tough as he thinks he is. Probably a hell of a lot tougher than anybody realizes. Somewhere between there. If there's anything that will keep him going, it's probably the fact that he is alone, he is black and he does believe he's going to survive.'

'Why?'

'He doesn't stop to think a lot. He acts. And every ounce of the man is muscle and anger.'

'Let me know what turns up on those two creeps from the bar.'

'Yes, sir.'

The phone was silent. Anderozzi dropped it back into the cradle. He would call the station and see what the fingerprints of the two hoods showed about their origin and background. He'd let the Commissioner know. Maybe he would call Shaft first. He wondered what the big, black bastard was doing. And to whom. He lay back down and snuggled against the warm, soft form of his wife.

Shaft thought that if he stopped to count all the things he had to do right then, right that minute without delay, he'd need the fingers of a centipede. This thing was taking all his time, all his energy, and, twice now, damn near all his life.

He couldn't even remember the last time he'd gone to the bathroom. He only thought about it now because the Scotch had been punching his kidneys and was putting the pressure of urgency on his bladder.

'Excuse me,' he said to the girl. 'You want a drink, there's a bottle of Scotch on top of the icebox and a bottle of vodka inside it.' She had dropped into the one club chair over near the window and kicked off her shoes. Apparently there was no question in her mind about why she was here, if the first thing she did was start taking off her clothes.

'It's all right, I'll wait. I have to go to the johnnie, too.'

He smirked, but turned away so she couldn't see, walking to the bathroom. In about ten minutes she was going to have more johnnie than she knew what to do with . . .

'What's your name?' he asked.

'Valerie.'

'Valerie?'

'Uh-huh.'

The name bothered him. It felt like a spider crawling across his memory.

Some village broad named Valerie shot up a fruit-cake painter a while back. It wasn't this one. She was in jail. He discarded the thought.

'Is your name Shaft or do they just call you that?'

'They just call me that. I'll be right back.'

He stared at the red, fatigue flushed whites of his eyes in the bathroom mirror, then got his first clear look at the collar of the shirt he had been wearing for what was now turning into three days. It was a ring of stain, the city dirt blended with sweat. He looked down at the gray trousers. They were a mess, too, and the Drago shine with which he had begun the involvement in this case no longer existed. It made him aware of how cruddy he felt from socks to collar. He had to get into the shower. Shaft squirted toothpaste on the brush, put it on the edge of the sink and stripped off the clothes. He didn't bother to hang them on the back of the bathroom door, just threw them in the corner of the bathroom. The .38 thumped when it hit the floor.

'Are you coming out?'

'Sure, sure. Just a minute.' He had forgotten all about her. Christ, this was too much. He picked up the toothbrush and stepped into the shower. He turned on the hot and cold faucets and jumped back to avoid the shock of the first cold spray out of the pipe. It got hot quickly and he leaned into it to adjust the temperature to just below scalding, scrubbing away at his teeth at the same time.

It was the best thing his body had felt for so long that he just stood there, letting the hot water beat upon him in a steaming cascade. Warm, wonderful water. He raised his face directly under the showerhead, about an inch from the holes through which a hundred streams of water gushed. He had to hold his breath. So warm, so soothing. It was all going to wash away and he was going to get out of the shower feeling fresh, strong and ready.

The touch on the small of his back startled him. He jumped and banged his skull on the showerhead, spinning around on the slippery porcelain with a roar.

'What in the hell?' he shouted.

'Did I scare you?' she asked.

The shower was pouring over his shoulder onto her body, rippling down its slopes and summits in roisterous rivulets. She was laughing and she had a bar of soap in her hand, moving to rub it across his chest.

'I hope you're not ticklish,' she said.

'That's it,' Shaft replied. 'That's my name. Ticklish.'

*　　*　　*

There were forty men in the room. Buford stood in the center of them. He was taller than most, more marked in his appearance than most. He stood on a steel and wood milk crate to emphasize both points. He was above them and he was the center of them. He turned slowly on the box, revolving to give each sector of the group a portion of his message and promise.

His right hand was raised and cocked like a pistol of flesh, pointing beyond their faces into their minds.

'How long you been waiting?' he demanded. The big voice, controlled and grim, starting out slowly, looking for the rhythm. 'How long you been waiting?' he repeated.

The response was an inarticulate rumble, a mixture of such muttered phrases as 'Four hundred years,' 'Too damn long,' and '*We* been waiting *forever*.'

'Too long,' Buford said. 'Too long,' continuing to revolve slowly like a mechanical doll turned by a device hidden in the milk crate. The voice leaped up to a roar: 'Well now we're not going to wait any longer! The time's come to do something more than talk about it.'

Forty throats roared assent.

'There's five voices missing tonight. Five black faces you ain't going to see no more. Five black bodies going to the grave today.'

Silence, echoing silence through the big warehouse chamber of exposed beams and concrete floor, torn cobwebs and a century of the accumulated dust that had seeped in through the rough construction. The crackling snuffle of men's shoes against the grime from which they have risen and in which they must walk. But heavy, great dark shrouds of silence.

Buford exploded it.

'*Goddamn, they are not going alone!*'

138

A deep, swelling roar, a hoarse growl of agreement and support.

'We're going to start now! We're going to wake up this city! We're going to take one a day! One pig cop! One black man who lives off his brother's misery! You know the plans! Now is the time we use them!'

A roar of assent, of eagerness. Restraint and planning had formed an uncomfortably tight leash. It was unhooked.

'The team leaders stay with me now. We have to talk. The rest of you keep cool until you hear from them.'

He continued to turn slowly on the box, trying to let his eyes touch on each face and bestow upon it the fulfillment of his promises and exhortations. All the beautiful, angry black faces shining with purpose and strength. Buford was troubled by a ragged scrap of thought about Shaft's talk of dealing. The faces before him told Buford that he did not need to deal. This was the power and it was his.

'Go,' he said. Why wasn't a man like Shaft with them for this? Where were men like Shaft when they were needed?

'This is why they call you Shaft,' she said, her soapy hands moving down his flanks. His were on her breasts. The lubricity of the soap made them almost impossible to hold. His fingers squeezed and glided across the slopes to the rigid nipples. He pressed and popped them softly like grapes through the tips of his thumbs and forefingers. Shaft wanted to ask her why some women had full, extended nipples, some had hardly any at all. It was no time for clinical questions. She began biting his chest, letting her teeth take little nips of the wet skin, hanging onto the moment before it became painful, then letting go and sliding her warm mouth an inch or so away. She had fingernails, too. Now her hands were moving up his sides to his shoulders, dragging the nails across the wet flesh.

'Baby,' he whispered to her, 'right now!'

She was small, so light. His arms went around her waist and he filled the cups of his hands with the rounded roll of her bottom, lifting her forward and upward. Her arms went around his neck and locked there drawing his face down to hers. Her legs parted and rose one at a time around his to lock behind his knees.

'Eeeeee,' she sighed as her body lowered on the rail of his flesh and he went into her naturally, perfectly with neither his hands nor hers guiding the slow thrust. 'Eeeeeee,' she keened again.

It was so smooth, Shaft was momentarily surprised. Was it the soap? Or the liquidity of her sex? Or that she was so open and eager for him? His body jerked compulsively in a spasmodic thrust and he drove deeply into her, as deeply as he could while her own body strained against him and his hands lifted her forward.

Standing there, bodies locked beneath the steaming spray, they began to seek the rhythm. Shaft bent his knees and reached out his left hand behind her to brace the stance with a grip on the towel rack. As his fingers tightened on the wooden bar, he felt her body begin to rise and fall in the movement of her pelvis, the slow and steady hammering of an impulse into ecstasy.

She had aroused him intensely. It was the surprise of it, having her come into the shower after him. It was also the soapy, slithering ritual of the bath and the whorish quality of her giving it to him. He wanted to let go, to drive and thrust without containment, then explode within and around her. It was frequently his style for the sometimes girl, the casual exercise. But for this one he would hold back. The way she had come to it deserved that. He would wait until she was screaming into his throat. Then he would let himself go and it would happen.

She began to moan. The hammer rose and fell more rapidly, spasmodically. She was only seconds away. The ridged bar of the towel rack bit into the flesh of his tightening hand. He never felt it.

'I'm coming!' she howled. So was Shaft. He had the feeling that they were pitching out of the shower onto the tile floor. But he didn't care.

The fact that there had been mistakes, serious mistakes, seeped through the pain in Carmen Caroli's crushed face with persistent anxiety. They had been his mistakes, he knew and he would pay a variety of penalties for them beyond what he was already suffering in physical damage and the shame of having been taken by the nigger, of having ended up in jail with his head wrapped in bandages and his life once again caught in the hamburger machine of the law. His mind moved slowly in review of those penalties as he sat on the edge of the bunk in the cell and stared at the steel-plate floor.

He wished he could lay back on the bunk and sleep. Each time he had tried, the throbbing in his head rose like the fury he felt when the cops came into the bar. He played out an imaginary conversation in his head, a dialogue with his brother Charlie, who would be the first to express the anger over what had happened.

'Why did he hit you with the bottle?' Charlie demanded.

'Who knows?' he said, sounding confused, dumb, because Charlie sometimes accepted his dumbness as an excuse. 'All niggers are crazy. As soon as the cop had the cuffs on me, he leans over and hits me with the bottle. Somebody must have tipped him that we were after him. It made him mad.'

'What do you mean, tipped him?'

It had been the wrong path, even in a fantasy. He always took the wrong path trying to explain to Charlie. To say that somebody tipped the nigger meant that one of the people who knew they were after the nigger had done it. And the only people who knew were Charlie and the other ones Charlie was with. Saying one of them caused it was more dangerous than getting caught. He always remembered these things too late. Now he had to weasel out of it.

'But how else would he know who we were?' He let his voice in the fantasy have more indignation than he would allow it if the confrontation had been real. But his fantasy was honest with him and Charlie snarled, just as he always did.

'Jesus Christ, with you two apes sitting in that saloon across from his apartment, how could he help but know who you were?'

Charlie was always right when they looked back on what had happened. That was why Charlie didn't trust him with much. He went on from the worst anxieties, facing his brother, to the lesser of them.

Three to five, he thought. He would probably do three to five on the gun rap. That was easy. Three to five was nothing unless the judge was wrong for him and came up one of those guys who makes speeches with each sentence so they can get their names in the papers. Then the three to five might be five to ten. Well, that was bad. The days eventually passed. They weren't such bad days. You always knew what was coming next in them. And, when they ran out, you could go home if you had a home.

Would he have a home? That penalty also crossed his mind with a dull trudge. He would lose Angela, for sure. Three to five, she might still be around. Five to ten, she'd have to go with somebody else. Who? He felt a twinge of jealousy. It made his head hurt. What difference did it make who? Somebody, anybody. There were guys around who wanted her and would take care of her. And Charlie, who would stay mad at him for almost ever. He would stay mad for the entire three to five. But would he stay mad for five to ten? If he did, if Charlie wasn't there when he got out, it might as well be twenty to life.

Carmen shuffled his feet across the steel floors without rising from the cot. The anxiety over Charlie's possible absence was too strong to continue. It drove his mind toward other concerns.

The girl. He thought about her, crapped out on the bed in the small room over Thompson Street. They had given her the jolt of the stuff that Charlie had brought around. Bang, in the arm, and she was out for six or eight hours.

'Shoot her in the ass, shoot her in the arm, what the hell difference does it make?' Charlie said. 'Just don't give her more than up to that little red line on the hypo. You understand?'

He understood that. He did it carefully, slowly. Why didn't Charlie just let him do that, sit there watching over the girl? He and Eddie read the papers and talked about the Mets and broads and some jobs they'd done. Why had Charlie taken them out of the room and sent them after the nigger?

'She'll be asleep for six hours for sure,' he said. 'Nothings going to happen to her. I'll stay. I want you to find this guy Shaft, this spade, and go over him good. Don't kill him, you understand? Just break a couple of things. His arm, his ankles maybe. I want to talk with him when he's slowed down some. You understand? You don't kill him. You just slow him down. Then you come back here straight.'

He had understood. It had been a simple job. But somehow he had blown it. Again. He wondered how mad Charlie was. He wondered what the big nigger was doing.

Chapter Nine

W HAT DO you do with them after you're done with them? Shaft pulled on a pair of black dungarees and padded out to the kitchen on bare feet. The floor was gritty. He wondered if he could work out some scheme with the chicks who woke up there to clean up part of the place before they left. The one in there on the bed could get the bathroom. There was a flood in there, water all over the place from the bouncing spray off the bouncing bodies. It had been her idea, hadn't it?

'You're crazy,' he said to himself. Aloud. He remembered one of them who was making coffee and cleaning house when he got out of bed one morning. It took three days to evict her. He went back to the bedroom while the coffee water was heating, plunged a hand into the shirt drawer looking for a black T-shirt, found one lurking in the scramble of underwear and socks, and pulled it over his head. He was not neat, he thought. That was one of the problems he had with living with himself. If he put everything in nice straight stacks, he'd know where everything was. Like, where the hell were two socks that resembled each other?

He looked at the sleeping girl. Spinners. She had turned the bathtub into a trampoline for the gymnastics of sex. That was all good. Different. He raised one foot, dusted off the sole with his hand and pulled on a sock, followed it with the other. He glanced at the luminous hands of his watch. Three, it glowed at him. She didn't take up much of the bed. But her presence took up part of his life. He had a lot to do. The kettle was making noises in the kitchen and he answered the whistle.

Standing at the stove under the blue glimmer of the circular fluorescent tube in the ceiling, watching the first drops of water move through the grounds and drip out as coffee, Shaft thought out the next step. He could go up to the jail first. Anderozzi would turn the official back, while he kicked the shit out of the two punks from the bar. Would they say anything? Probably not. They would scream for lawyers and yell about brutality. They might not even know anything.

Or he could ask Anderozzi to put him onto a Mafiaoso don and offer a quick trade, his testimony against the pair for information about Beatrice. No, on two points. No Italian cop, not even Anderozzi, would admit to a Mafia connection and, two, nobody would trade anything for those two fools. They were expendable. That wasn't a trade anybody would make because that wasn't what they wanted.

Well, what did they want? The drug traffic in Spanish Harlem. If it was as simple as that, he could probably give it to them. But nothing was simple. He poured a cup of coffee, went back into the living room and set the cup on a table while he went into the bathroom and retrieved the pile of clothes from the corner. Soggy, mush. He might as well throw the gray suit away. The gun was damp. It was a fat, snub-nose revolver, blue-black and gleaming with a light coat of oil. Somebody must have taken care of it. Maybe the owner of the bar. He stuck it in his waistband, just to the center of his left hipbone. Twice now, attempts had been made to kill him. The steel in his belt was reassuring. He rethought the encounters with the gunmen. They wanted to kill him the first time for sure. But maybe not last night. Wouldn't they have been more efficient? Or wouldn't they have sent somebody more capable?

The coffee burned his tongue. He got the beans at a little

shop called McNulty's a few blocks away on Christopher Street. French Roast. You ground your own coffee, and it tasted like coffee. When he remembered to get the beans, it was all good. When he forgot, it was instant and awful. He flicked out the light, opened the venetian-blind slats and looked out on the street while he drank it. He felt invisible. A black man in black pants and shirt with a black gun in his belt. The coffee cup was white. Disembodied in the blackness, it floated back and forth to his lips.

The money from the other back pocket of the gray pants was a wet and lumpy bundle. He had dropped the envelope on the small, circular wood table that stood between two windows in the kitchen. He needed a safety deposit box with night service. He picked up the envelope, turned to the refrigerator and pulled open the door. Shaft held the door with his elbow, pulled down the panel that sealed off the freezer. It needed defrosting badly. There were two or three cartons of vegetables, a couple half-empty pints of ice cream, four trays of ice cubes. He slipped two one hundred dollar bills out of the envelope and stashed it behind the Seabrook Farms package of green peas and little white onions, then moved the ice cream in front of that. He'd have to thaw it before he spent any more of it.

One more cup of coffee. Shaft glanced at his watch again. Three-ten. He had about half an hour. Half an hour before the bars would close down, the unquenchably thirsty would stumble out onto the Village sidewalks for the mumbling meander home and everything except cops, freaks and all-night coffee shops would call it a night. Half an hour. It wasn't much. It was all he had.

He padded back into the bedroom, looked at the girl again. She hadn't moved. What do you do with them after you're done with them? Let them sleep. Hopefully, she would get up and go home in time to change for work. Hopefully, she worked someplace. He felt a moment's concern. What day was it? If last night was Friday, it was now Saturday and she'd want to sleep until noon. Shit! What day was it? He counted them on the fingers of his memory, one at a time, trying to move events into agreement with the calendar. It came out Thursday night into Friday morning. He felt relieved, so relieved that he leaned over and set the clock radio for seven o'clock. He usually woke up to an FM station, WBAI, where there was a chronic bitcher at the microphone each morning, playing unusual records and complaining about life and the world. He turned the dial to a hard-rock station and told himself he was doing the girl a favor, fixing it so she would get up in time to go home and change before she went to work. It was a lie. He knew it. He turned the volume dial up. It would blow her out into Jane Street. Short romances were the best ones.

Shaft moved quietly from the radio to the closet, squatted to grope through the shoes in a rough line on the floor, until he found the black crepe-soled oxfords, then got the black oiled silk jacket off the hanger and thrust his arms into it. Was there anything else? He checked out the pockets one by one for keys, money, wallet, handkerchief, cigarettes. Cigarettes. Where were they? There was a pack on the bedside table. His or hers, he didn't remember. Marlboros. Hers. He put the box in one of the slash pockets of the jacket and turned to leave.

Was there anything in the place the chick could steal? Unless she got behind the green peas and pearl onions to his stash in the freezer, there wasn't anything worth the trouble of carting out of the place. He looked at the watch. Three-fifteen. Not much time. He looked at the girl. If he wanted her, he could always find her, he thought, and tiptoed out the door, zipping up the jacket over the bulk of the pistol and noting that it didn't bulge enough to attract attention. There wasn't much time for any of them and there was only one way to do this. The hard way.

Chapter Ten

S HAFT IGNORED the elevator and walked down the three flights of stairs, moving quietly, pausing at infrequent intervals to listen to the night noises of sleeping buildings. If there was anyone with him, it was only the ghosts of his imagination. He was too much a realist to listen to their voices. He thought of going down into the basement of the apartment house, quieting the super's dog with a pat on the head or a kick in the teeth and slipping out of the building through the rear, the narrow service alley between apartments and then over the fence on Hudson Street. There was less risk in going out the front door. A chance cop, wandering the empty streets in pursuit of his own night-shift boredom, was a greater danger than ambush at the front door. He couldn't run on top of a wrought-iron fence. He couldn't shoot back at a cop who caught him playing cat burglar and gave him a warning shot through the forehead.

But at the front door of the building, the second entrance off the foyer that was opened only by a key or buzzer from the individual apartments, he turned off the foyer light with the wall switch in the hallway. He didn't wait for the possibility that someone would notice and be alerted, but stepped into the blackness in a quick stride, pulled open the Jane Street door and put himself into the street, moving east to the right, past the long row of brownstones toward the foot of Eighth Avenue.

Shaft moved quickly. He was march-stepping through the

few seconds it took to reach Eighth Avenue. He went around the newsstand corner in a dog trot and crossed Eighth Avenue diagonally at Twelfth Street where it comes up the side of Abingdon Square, the pointless little triangle that nobody remembers, nobody uses. He was jogging when he turned into Bleecker Street, angling off Eighth at Bank Street and plunged into the soft underbelly of Village antique shops.

The small collections of jumble and dust glowed at him under the fragile cowardice of night lights. The doorways were dark and silent, emptier than the hopes that lived behind them. Still he searched them all. It was part of knowing, being aware, getting ready. It felt good to move the hard, solid body this way and he was aware of the blood beginning to churn through muscle and tissue in a rhythm that is the heartbeat and the joy of the natural athlete.

Where had the idea come from? Shaft asked himself as he went past Christopher Street toward Seventh Avenue. It just came, that's all. Its mother was desperation and its father was anger. The seed of it was planted back in the No Name when he realized what was happening and that he had somehow to change the pattern of it, take a positive role in it. He couldn't live and he couldn't work in the context of dealing for his life everytime he turned a corner. The focus had to change, to go back to the girl. Where was she? How did he get her back? What did they demand as the price of this? And how did he serve and survive as the broker of such a transaction? There was only one way.

There was traffic on the broad artery of Sixth Avenue. Where the hell did it come from at three-twenty in the morning? He stopped and watched it flow north, cabs and cars and three or four trucks, until the light changed and he ran across the street. He picked up on the cop standing around the doorway to the grocery store on the corner and wondered if he was going to be stopped and frisked. They did this to black men and white men who came running out of the Greenwich Village night. They might even have questions for little old ladies who came jogging across Sixth Avenue in black dungarees and black jackets. But the cop was tired or bored or, more likely, worried about being alone; he watched Shaft without a move to stop him.

Maybe the man even recognized him. Shaft had come down this street a hundred times on nights that ended at the Village Gate. Or was it that the cop was alone? Lately, over the last two or three years, they made their confrontations in pairs. What was the line? The place is so dangerous even the muggers go in pairs. So one cop didn't want to stop one black man jogging across the thoroughfare, heading Christ knows where on a quiet spring night and risk the confrontation, the explosion.

Bleecker suddenly turned Italian after Sixth Avenue. Here, the bakeries, the funeral parlor that looked like a remnant of a Hollywood movie about Chicago gangsters, the butcher shops garlanded with fat sausages, sweet and hot, and the delicatessen windows crammed with cans of olive oil, tomatoes and petrifying strands of pasta – they stood timeless ethnic defiance of beat, hip and yip, of black, brown and bruised. To the north, to Shaft's left, Thompson, MacDougal and Sullivan Streets sprayed bead and bangle shops toward Washington Square. To the south, to Shaft's right, they gave refuge to small apartment houses, to Italian restaurants, the bars, holding the line between Bleecker and West Houston Street for an older, quieter Greenwich Village and the people who really owned it.

There were still some people around. Standing, walking, talking. Just staring into the night. The spooked, the stoned and the sleepless. Half of them were probably narcs, pursuing the crushed minds of the other half or selling them desperation by the ounce. The narcotics cop was a special breed, half pursuer, half pusher. How did they live with it? Shaft had wondered. But not at that moment. He kept running. He turned south into Sullivan Street, traveling a memory map of where the places were.

Petrone's Fine Cuisine was the first, a splotch of neon about a third of the way down the block. He jogged to the door, pulled it open and stepped in. The bartender was startled into paralysis over the tub in which he was washing glasses. His face was black clouds of suspicion and hatred for the dark intruder who had come out of the night into the quiet of his closing minutes.

'Hey, man,' Shaft said, leaning both hands on the brim of the bar, neither raising nor lowering his voice but speaking slowly and clearly, 'where the hell is the headquarters of the Mafia?'

The bartender's Adam's apple bobbled; the man was trying to swallow hard on a dry throat. He was silent.

'The Mafia,' Shaft repeated. 'Where do they hang their guns?'

When voice finally came to the barman, it was cramped, squeezed and scraped.

'You better get the hell out of here,' he croaked.

Shaft nodded, his face furrowed in puzzlement, a man who could not understand why he was not understood.

'Okay,' he said. 'But you see any Mafia people around here, you tell them John Shaft just dropped by to say hello.'

He banged out the door hurriedly. The place had been all but empty, yet he felt that a hundred sets of eyes had taken in his presence. He was smiling when he got to the sidewalk. He felt the air on his teeth as he let himself go and sprinted to the corner of West Houston. There, it was the Casa Mario and the bartender was talking with a tired, fat waitress who viewed Shaft as if she had apprehended him urinating on her Christmas tree.

'We're all closed down,' the bartender said nervously.

'That's all right,' Shaft replied, walking close to them, letting the terror of their fantasies work for him. 'I don't drink. I'm looking for the main office of the Mafia. Around here somewhere.'

They didn't say anything at all. They could only stare at the apparition that had come to profane the sacred fiefdom of fear and respect. To curse the church was one matter and an understandable one, if a man were so emotionally moved; to challenge the true god who laid a blanket of suppression and protection over the community, this was unthinkable.

'Ah,' Shaft said, 'you don't know either. Well you tell them John Shaft is trying to find them. Okay?'

He was almost high, giddy by the time he reached the sixth or seventh of the places. Maybe it was the oxygen being sucked into his bloodstream by the running. His body felt warm and all joined together, his mind as bright and burning as a blue-flame acetelyne torch cutting through plate steel. He was high on the stakes in the gamble. He had never bet more than his life on anything.

'Listen,' he said to the last of them, a short, round, owl-eyed Sicilian who seemed to be edging toward a drawer under the cash register until he noticed that Shaft's jacket gaped at the zipper over the butt of a revolver. 'Listen, when you hear from them, tell them I'm over at the corner of Bleecker and MacDougal, waiting to talk.' He took the gun out of the waistband and laid it side down on the bar, pointing nowhere. 'Tell them this is a business call from John Shaft.'

It was a gesture, about as meaningful as throwing snowballs at a police car. It said defiance, without breaking anything. The one thing they couldn't do was improvise. And they had no sense of humor. Behind each move, each piece of cunning, was the certain prospect that somebody would go to prison or his death for each mistake. So it had to be played by plan, not by ear. Now he was demanding, irritating by his presence, that they improvise. That reduced it to finding out just what in the hell *he* wanted. This became merely a gun, one gun he had put down on the bar only when they found out what he intended to do with it and prevented it.

Shaft glanced at the clock on the bar wall, a tasteless white-faced clock with big numerals. It was as out of place in the pink-light, red-leather, gold-stucco decor of the bar as he was. It said four o'clock. Time was always ten minutes fast in saloons. The promise of the whisky was a lie; so was the limit on calling for more to seek the truth. It was almost four o'clock and he had done enough, said enough.

Shaft covered the gun with the broad, scarred hand and scooped it back into the waistband of his slacks. The message was so loud and clear that it must be echoing through every rathole in the Village – and a lot of plush, quiet bedrooms in the soft suburbs across the Hudson in New Jersey. They'd be talking about it in Palermo in an hour.

'I'm going over to the Borgia,' he said. 'I'll wait there.'

'Don't hold your breath,' the bartender advised with the cold farewell of an undertaker.

One last sprint. Shaft made his legs go as fast as they could toward the light-blanketed corner of Bleecker and MacDougal. By now, he was a pigeon on the wing. It had taken him about half an hour. That was enough for one of the important ones to place an order for his death. Time enough for one of the unimportant ones to get the gun out of the drip tank under the refrigerator, out of the crib mattress in the infant's room, out of the oilskin wrapper under the dirt in the window box – to get the gun and come after him. He ran with a touch of fear on his driving body and became angry with himself when he sensed it. Were they already there behind the parked cars and in the night-darkened doorways? Were they coming at him behind the headlights moving down the street?

'Fuck it!' he said aloud. Come and try it. Come and deal with me in these dark streets. I know the dark streets and the dark ways and their sudden violence the same as you. He doubted if anybody but a jungle sniper with an infra-red scope on a rifle could have gotten him as he ran. The last man who had tried that had done it from a perch above the swamp at Kinong – and came down head first into the ooze. Try, he thought, try. The fear went away, but he was not reassured until he reached the lights of Bleecker once more, turned toward the outdoor lanterns and awnings of the late-night espresso house, the Cafe Borgia.

It was almost closing time in the coffee house, too, the hissing espresso machine ready to sigh into silence as the pastries were put on trays for a rest under refrigeration. The cop on the corner ignored him, played whirly-bird with the nightstick and the thongs that held it. If the cop had gotten through the night on that corner without trouble, there was no point in looking for it now in the reasons why this black man had come quietly to the coffee house on the corner. The cop sauntered north into MacDougal Street for another patrol of the hurdy-gurdy, sideshow block between Bleecker and West Third, where the freaks got out on the sidewalks, mingling with the marks.

There were only four or five people in the Borgia, scattered like spring raindrops around the marble tables, in the big square room framed in mediocre murals in pre-impressionist-house-painter awful. A long-haired boy and two short-haired girls, staring dully into the bottoms of espresso cups, waiting for the night to end or hoping that it would somehow begin. Shaft had the feeling that it never would for most of them, either way. They were a weak, white generation who couldn't stand the slightest test in the brutality of becoming people. They had opted for the nothing of their lives with the momentary relief of the uppers and the downers that they could swallow or smoke. Cop-outs. There was a couple over in the corner by the window that peered out at Bleecker, middle-aged people who seemed more unlikely in the setting, neither stoned nor smashed, but just people. Insomniacs, maybe. Just people in tweed jackets and wool slacks and linen dresses. Both kinds of them had a place there, he thought. But did he?

It was the same question in the approach of the slender, long-haired blond girl wearing a little white French maid's apron over her Madras print dress. This was the kind of job the actresses took, waiting tables through the night, in exchange for time and money for making the casting office rounds during the day. Now she was making the rounds of the ashtrays and yesterday's canoli crumbs. There was a guy behind the counter in the far corner away from the door, fiddling with the espresso machines. That was the lot. It left a room of twenty or thirty small marbletop tables looking like a grove of giant toadstools, pushing against each other and struggling to survive in the dim, damp cave of the room.

Which one? He moved through the thigh-nudging labyrinth toward the far corner. Next to the counter, a small round table with a view. He could sit there, back against the wall and see what was coming from any direction. If that made any difference. The plate-glass windows of the Borgia were open screens onto a piece of MacDougal on one side, Bleecker on the other.

'Espresso,' he told the girl who put down the menu in front of him, then picked it up on the note of finality in his voice. Shaft wondered how she would react when the place exploded. She was only nineteen or twenty. She looked calm and controlled. It might be fatigue. Crash, bang and slam the world down around her pink ears suddenly and she could turn into a banshee of hysteria. It might happen. He hoped she didn't get hurt. He was more concerned with keeping himself from getting hurt.

When the girl's back was turned as she got his espresso, Shaft slipped the .38 out of the belt where it was poking into his groin. He settled it in the lapcreases of his slacks, then pulled the marble table two or three inches closer. There was no out now. Shaft told himself that he was either one of the coolest of men or the dumbest of bastards to have done it. When the thoughts leaped across the electric circuit of his head, his hand touched the pistol for reassurance. Shit. That wouldn't buy five seconds of deep breathing. It would just give them something else to think about. One thing, nobody advertised a murder. Not even his.

'What?' the girl asked, putting the cup of hot mud on the table.

'Got any lemon peel?' He had been talking to himself. Aloud.

'Sure,' she said, turning back to the counter. He was embarrassed. Goddamnit, here he sat in a dingy fucking coffee joint at four o'clock in the morning with a bunch of cartoons painted on the walls around him, a gun in his lap, the Mafia about to shoot his ass off, some chick in his apartment who'd probably walk off with his clock-radio as the price of pussy. He was tired. He didn't want the brown scum in the cup on the table, he didn't want to talk with anybody or play games with his life or anybody else's. He wanted to be the last man in the world for about ten days to drink a bottle of Johnnie Walker all by himself, walk around in circles until he fell down on the ground to just sleep, sleep, sleep.

'Do you want anything else?' she asked. 'We're closing in a little while.'

The world was closing forever in a little while if he had been as stupid as he seemed to himself.

'Hell, I don't even want what I got.'

She was puzzled. 'Is there something wrong with the espresso? I'll have him make another cup.'

She moved to take it away.

'No, no,' he said, reaching out, touching her arm lightly to stop her. He smiled. She didn't pull her arm away from the leprosy of his blackness. There was a whole generation like her and another coming behind them. They didn't see the color, they felt the touch. 'No, it's just fine. I was thinking about eight other things.'

'It's late, I guess,' she said.

'It sure as hell is,' he agreed. But not for her. He was agreeing for himself. His eyes were on the door. There were three men coming through it. They had apparently approached the place from the diagonally opposite corner, rather than pass by the windows.

Shaft's hand floated as casually as yesterday's promises to the pistol butt in his lap. He hoped he looked like a man who was about to scratch his crotch, if they were looking. They didn't seem to be, any more than most people look at the occupants of a restaurant they are entering. If he tipped the marble table in front of him, it covered most of the vital parts, he thought. He wondered how tough marble was. It looked chipped and scarred by the ashtrays and cups being dropped on it. Marble wasn't as hard as bullets.

They moved down the MacDougal Street side of the room, three burly men in murky dark suits. They gathered themselves like a pawnbroker's grapes around the last table in the line, two of them facing him, one of them with his back to Shaft. Whoever they were, they wanted a corner view of the room. Three salesmen out chasing Village pussy and failing, as almost all of them failed? Or three men come to deal with him?

The blond girl went to see what they wanted of the Borgia's

commodities. Shaft watched her tail twitch across the room beneath the Madras print. It wasn't the worst way to die, staring at a girl's ass. He pinched the lemon peel and dropped the pulpy remains of the rind into the quicksand in the cup. He began to sense something about the men at the table. They were hard around the edges. They weren't salesmen. It was a hardness that came to men who are dipped into the substream that flows between the city's veneer of civilized coexistence with its violence. Cab drivers and bartenders had the edge. So did cops and cutthroats. And Shaft had it. It came to them when they were hung out to dry.

He was distracted by a movement at the door. Some goddamned beautiful seat he'd chosen for himself. Here came three more of them and he hadn't seen anybody pass the windows yet. The new arrivals were illustrations ripped out of the same book. Ordinary suits, ordinary-looking men. But hard. And they seemed to be looking only for a table – that one over in the other corner on the same side of the wall where he sat, only up near the window. They sat the same way, two against the wall, one with his back to the room.

That made a triangle in the square room. He had one corner, they had two others and the door took the fourth. He never felt lonelier, he never felt more vulnerable. There was no way out except through the line that could be drawn between the clusters of men. There was no way out at all for John Shaft.

The middle-aged couple paid the blond, took their change and drifted out. The long-haired kid and the short-haired girls up front just sat there. Four-seventeen, his watch said. What do you do now, yo-yo? it asked him. He looked at the blond passing by with the order from the three most recent arrivals and pointed at his empty cup. She nodded. What he would do was drink coffee and wait – wait for the door to open and his man to come in. It did. So did the man, the one he had been looking for this night, the one who had been looking for him. He spotted Shaft instantly and came directly across the room to his table, not slowly, not quickly, but as a man with business to attend to, even at four-eighteen o'clock on a spring morning in Greenwich Village.

'I sure am glad you look like a wop punk,' Shaft said in greeting, the .38 under the table fixed on what he guessed was the position of the caller's belt buckle. 'We might have missed each other in the crowd.'

'I'd know you anywhere, nigger,' the man said, pulling out a chair to sit down opposite him. 'How about a nice slice of watermelon with your coffee?'

They smiled at each other. It occurred to Shaft that there were other people in the world as hard as he was. They had come off the same production line of the same mill. Now they were colliding head on. He could hear steel tearing against steel, a muted screech below the murmur of conversation at the other tables in the room.

'They put too much garlic in it here,' Shaft said. 'And they don't like you to spit seeds on the other customers.'

Chapter Eleven

LIEUTENANT VICTOR ANDEROZZI sat on the edge of his bed, gazing down on the pond of darkness in which he dangled his slender, almost delicate feet. His body called for him to topple back into the rumpled scramble of sheets and blankets to seek out the indentation that had been molded by the weight of his body. His conscience told him to get up and get dressed. He wasn't sure who was going to win. He wasn't sure he cared. Shaft had ripped it good this time and the silly bastard deserved whatever was going to happen to him. The only trouble with that was it might be the *last* thing that ever happened to Shaft and he, Anderozzi, would be partially responsible for it.

His wife was snoring. Goddamnit, everybody in the world was snoring except Victor Anderozzi. Even half the midnight-to-eight shift was cooping in discreetly parked patrol cars or snoozing on desks in the back end of the precinct houses. The other half was trying to keep John Shaft alive through the night. He thought briefly of waking up his wife to do her part in that effort by making him some coffee. He also thought briefly of waking up the Police Commissioner to see if he wanted to do *his* part. In fact, he wished he had the button to the biggest goddamned siren in the world, so he could push it and wake up *everybody* in the whole fucked-up city of New York to have them do *their* part in it. Instead, he reached for another cigarette, struck a tiny torch that hurt his eyes and made grotesque shadows of the life he lived and the way he lived it.

Leaning over his knees in the darkness, Anderozzi tried to puzzle out Shaft's movements. He had been sitting on the edge of the bed since the first phone call, informing him that the black man was running loose among the swamp guineas of the Village. What the hell was he doing? They didn't know; he was just out of his apartment and running. Well, goddamnit, was he out jogging in the middle of the night? Don't get mad at us, Lieutenant, he's just running down the streets. Watch him, then. Okay. Four minutes later they called again. Shaft was running from bar to bar. What the hell was he doing? Robbing them? They didn't know. Goddamnit, find out! Fast! The next call came seven minutes later. They had found out what Shaft was doing. Anderozzi let them hang onto the silence while he thought. He was resented in the department for his position as neither cop nor commander, but the man who worked for the Commissioner. When he thought for the Commissioner, both cop and captain waited for the results. And what did he think? That Shaft was finally going to get killed. The phone call after this one would be to say that the meat-wagon crew was scraping the pieces of him off a wall someplace.

'All right,' he said finally, 'if they make contact with him, if there's a legitimate approach to him by anybody, let it happen and stay out of it. Is that clear? Stay out of it. But until it's certain, stay with him every inch of the way. He's crazy, unpredictable and smart.'

Anderozzi might have added stubborn, largely unpleasant in the extreme toward any form of authority, momentarily independent and violent in his response to abuse, real or imagined. But why bother to tell them? The only thing worse than a dumb cop who knew nothing was a smart-ass who knew too much. They would find out what Shaft was like if they didn't follow instructions. So he just hung up the receiver.

'How about a cup of coffee?' Anderozzi said to the inert form

162

of his wife. There wasn't the slightest interruption in the pattern of her snore. He hadn't expected one. He got up, groped for his robe on a chair and headed for the kitchen, fighting to get his arms through the rayon tubes of sleeves without ripping them. It was four forty-two and apparently his day was beginning. The coffee pot was clean and empty, sitting on a cold burner of the white gas range. At least he didn't have to screw around getting rid of the grounds. He almost forgave her for sleeping through his anxiety about Shaft. One spoon, two spoons, three spoons, Shaft spoons. Shaft. What in God's name are you going to do next?

'Who the hell are you anyhow?' Shaft asked.

'What the hell difference does it make?' the man replied. 'You wanted to see somebody. I'm here.'

'You got the girl?'

'You always drink coffee with your left hand?'

Shaft smiled. So did the man. He felt a little foolish. He put the .38 back in his lap and brought his right hand out on top of the table.

'You got the girl?'

'Sure.'

'How do I know?'

'I'll show you. Come on.'

He started to get up from the bent-steel ice-cream-parlor chair, scraping it back along the tiles a couple of inches.

'Wait a minute,' Shaft said. 'You'll show me when I want to see her.'

'Okay.' The man shrugged. He couldn't care less. He greeted the arrival of the waitress with a bright, hard smile. 'Hello, sweetheart.' She responded with a twitching at the corner of the mouth. 'Give me whatever my friend is having.'

The girl was upset. It was closing time and she had eight

grown men and three ungrown hippies to deal with. She wanted to go home, not back and forth to the hissing espresso apparatus.

He turned the hard, dying smile on Shaft.

'Girls like that,' he said. 'Soft, but they got good muscles. I used to like to take a girl like that, kid who maybe needed a couple of bucks or a square meal, or maybe she was just lonely, and run her through every position she ever dreamed about, you know? All in one night. Fuck their brains out. They been fooling around with these fags and spades around here and · they think that's sex. But each time you make it a little rougher, a little stranger. They go out of their minds. Pretty soon they're screaming when they get it and screaming when they don't get it. They don't know the difference. They're begging, but they don't know what they're begging for. You got the picture? She's rolling around the bed screaming, "Please, please, please." So you give it to her as hard as you can and all the time she keeps screaming, "Please, please, please." When you stop, when you get done, she keeps right on going. "Please, please, please."'

Charles Caroli, whose brother's bottle-broken head lay uneasily on a rubber-covered pallet in the city jail, turned his dark and sharply etched face toward the waitress. She was leaning back against the counter, simultaneously resting her feet, staying ready for the next summons from one of the tables and toting up checks on a green-lined pad with the stub of a pencil. He waited until she looked up, motioned her to the table.

'Yes, sir.'

'Listen, you want to catch the show at the Gate some night? Nina Simone . . .'

He was a vital-looking young man, somewhere around thirty, the carefully tailored pin-stripe suit in muted gray

164

working quietly off a gray shirt and darkly crimson tie. No jewelry showing, but a gold Patek Phillippe with a gold mesh band glistened somewhere beneath the cuff on his left wrist. Shaft glanced up at the girl. He caught a fragment of her uncertainty.

'I'm usually so tired I just . . .' The apology trailed off into indecision. She really wanted to go. She just wasn't sure she wanted to go with Charles Caroli. What did he want of her that he couldn't find elsewhere? Shaft felt her bend toward the flattery of the invitation. She fielded a thousand propositions in a week, but this was the first invitation. A good-looking young man had invited her to a nightclub three blocks away, not to his bed, whatever that may be.

'Think about it,' Caroli said, letting her off the hook. 'We'll be here awhile.'

Please, please, please. Shaft thought of Beatrice. He had never so much as seen the girl. His vague idea of what she looked like came from Knocks' description and a small snapshot that the mountainous gangster had given him. Shaft had left it on his desk. He didn't need it. The picture Charles Caroli had given him was clear. A small, black body writhing on a bed, sobbing, 'Please, please, please.'

Caroli he could kill. It would be simple. The man was hard, cold and sure under the soft gray suit. Prison hard. Mob hard. Gutter hard. Killer hard. A different kind of tempering than most people understood. But Shaft felt harder. He was sure he could kill Caroli with his hands, as soon as they got out of this place and walked down the dark tunnels of the Greenwich Village streets. One shot with either hand would take him out. Then he could stand on his throat and kill him. For a second, it was all he could think, a wish superimposed on the vision of the black girl on the bed. A vision of all the bodies on all the beds. Please, please, please.

And then what would he do? Kick the corpse into somebody's hallway and go back to his apartment content, satisfied – and wondering where Beatrice was and how to get her back. Sometimes, it was so easy to kill. Sometimes, it was so hard to think. Caroli was smiling at him. Caroli was that smart. He knew what was happening in Shaft's head.

'Where is she?'

'Like I said, I'll show you. Right around the corner. Whenever you're ready.'

'You want to deal?'

'With you?' He let his head roll back in a short, sharp laugh. 'Christ, you're a messenger boy. What kind of a deal can I make with you?'

Shaft's right hand fell off the table, back into his lap.

'You can make one right now to stay alive, you silly motherfucker. I just got to the limit of you.'

Caroli's world was crowded with psychopaths. The possibility that Shaft was one of them penetrated his arrogance. His smile slid off the side of his face like a rejected panhandler shuffling across cold concrete.

'That won't get you anything,' he said.

'Don't ever be sure. It's all we're talking about right now.'

'All right. All right. So we talk about what we want. It isn't much. We want Harlem.'

'Spanish Harlem,' Shaft said.

'Harlem,' Caroli corrected.

'You ain't going to get it.'

'Maybe yes, maybe no. But that's the deal.'

'Do you know what's going on up there? With the people?'

'I don't want to. We know how much there is and how it's moving. That's enough to know.'

'Not anymore, it isn't.'

166

There was an edge of impatience, boredom in Caroli's voice. 'I told you what the deal was.'

'For Beatrice.'

'Is that her name? We call her . . .' He glanced to Shaft's arm, resting in his lap. He reconsidered. 'For Beatrice.'

It was very simple. Most basic things are, Shaft thought. When you scraped away the complexities and looked at them, you realized that they had been added to the basic issues between men by their fears, greeds and maybe lusts. But the issues remained the same. Simple. All you had to do was get down to them. They had Beatrice and they wanted Harlem. One for one. Knocks Persons had Harlem and he wanted Beatrice. One for one. What about the five men who had died in the thunderstorm of bullets that fell on Amsterdam Avenue? Well, what about them? What about the fact that the attempt had been to kill Shaft? Well, what about it? Those things happened. They had some reasons, maybe good reasons at the time and bad reasons now, but reasons. What difference did these make now? As men, they were down to the issues at last. A realist could see that the rest of it was meaningless, pointless.

'You consider the possibility,' Shaft asked, 'that maybe there is no room to deal, that maybe we just turn it over to the law?'

'Sure,' Caroli said. 'We're ready to handle it that way. Like you can call them right now. Or so can I. Like we can call over those six bastards on either side of us and ask them to sit in on this . . .'

They had to be police, the clusters at the tables in the opposite corners. He had been concentrating so hard on Caroli, his own wild plan for making the contact, that he hadn't picked up on them. How goddamned stupid he could get sometimes. He had wondered if they were mob, not law.

167

'. . . and I'll give them the address. They go up there and what do they find? They find this black broad stoned out of her head with about six needles in the place and eight, ten decks of horse sprinkled around. Oh, yeah, she's got needle marks all over her arms and ass. We do that and they make a great score. Maybe pack this broad off to the can for about twenty, thirty years. You want to call them or you want me to do it?'

Of course they were cops. But how did they get there? He was angry and embarrassed at their lumpish presence. Anderozzi, or somebody, didn't trust him to bring it off. So they sent help. Unrequested, unwanted and unneeded help. Most likely, they had been told to watch Shaft, he thought. That was the limit of the imagination.

His mind went back to the acid Caroli was dripping on him. Beatrice. Goodbye, Beatrice. You are going to the can for a twenty-year Federal narcotics rap. And Knocks will sit in his leather bathtub weeping over you until the hippo bulk of him has been squeezed dry by the weight of pain. What then? Who will have won? They will. They will have weakened and worried him and in that found the flaw. Shaft decided then, sitting in judgment on the unlikely bench of a marble-top table in a Greenwich Village coffee house, that the empire of Knocks Persons was finished. As huge and powerful as it might be, now it had to topple. It was human. And all things human could perish.

'You got him pretty good,' Shaft said. 'Either way.'

Caroli was smart enough not to show his pride about the concession.

'It looks that way,' he said.

The .38 in Shaft's hand weighed a hundred pounds of futility. He slipped it back into the folds of the oilskin jacket and the waistband of his pants. The muzzle pinched the flesh of his groin and the inflexible steel made him sit up straighter. It, too, was an unwanted, unneeded embarrassment now. What the hell good was it?

'I'll see what Knocks says,' he agreed. 'But I think you got a deal.'

'I think we have.'

'But let's keep the game honest. Let's go see Beatrice. If she's alive, if it's like you say it is, that's the way it'll be. If she's not, if it's something else, I'm going to put six buttonholes up and down your spine.'

'I got to make a call first,' Caroli said, ignoring the threat, glancing around for the pay phone that hung like a big, black bug on the wall near the restrooms. He started to get up. Shaft stopped him with a shake of his hand.

'No calls,' he said. 'We just get up and go.'

The racketeer hesitated, then nodded, pushing back the chair.

'All right, we just go.'

Shaft thought about saying goodbye to the six cops, maybe sending his regards to Anderozzi. But they were such humorless bastards. Most of them could only laugh at the sight of blood. He thought also of stopping to tell them to stay the hell out of what was happening. That, too, would be futile. They did what they were told to do and some of what they were expected to do. Shaft had no influence over that and knew it. So he could only follow Caroli out of the Borgia, tossing a couple of dollars on the table top for the girl. He glanced at the three hippies sitting in the window booth. They were probably cops, too, he thought.

Caroli held the door for him, waved to the left, up toward the Gate. Shaft was glad the sonofabitch hadn't been able to make the girl agree to a date. Probably he never wanted one. But just in case, Shaft was just-in-case glad. It was about five o'clock. Even these streets, these last of all New York streets to become empty in any night as the wound of the day closed, were at last deserted. The two men were almost an intrusion into the new quiet of them. They walked quickly, without talking, the white man in the business suit slightly in the lead of the black man in his black uniform. At Thompson Street, they turned right, more or less south as the gerrymander streets of the Village wander. This was even quieter, emptier. A street with the feeling of loss behind the crabbed, crinkled façade of small windows set in blotched red brick, grated with steel and iron like the windows of a jail.

'Here,' said Caroli. A building distinguishable from all the others in the block only by the Chinese laundry on the sidewalk level, curtained and hidden from the street by dark, loosely hanging material on bamboo rods and a cluster of ferns in one corner. It occurred to Shaft as he turned into the building that Chinese laundry windows were always full of ferns because they were so dark and damp.

The lobby door was unlocked, without a buzzer system to control hallway access. The tenants must have made some exciting discoveries from time to time, Shaft thought. Or maybe the tenants were all like Caroli – and the hallway lurkers wished they had lurked elsewhere. The thought amused him. He visualized someone attempting to mug a man who had grown up mugging the world, maiming it, killing it. In such hallways as these, in the alleys around the corner.

But Shaft was thinking mostly of where they were and how the building was situated in the middle of Thompson Street, what the inside layout would be. There was at least some light in it, a glare thrown by an uncovered bulb in a cockeyed fixture dangling from the high ceiling of the entrance hall. It glared on a long, narrow set of stairs rising to the gloomy darkness of the floors above, while the downstairs hall, a sliver of cracked and dirty tiles, ran past the stairway toward the rear of the building. There were plain brown doors with enameled tin numbers nailed to them – one and two – on either side of the hallway. Presumably there were similar doors for three and four down the dark hall. Shaft couldn't tell in the darkness. But it was likely. The owners of these old cakes of decay and filth cut them into as many slices as possible. It was the way to beat the overhead, it was the way to get rich. Harlem or Greenwich Village, landlords were all the same. Like wolves everywhere. The people they were devouring tasted just as good.

He couldn't see down the hallway and he had to follow Caroli, who took off up the stairs quickly, half running, one at a time. Like one of those prancing faggots who dance up the stairs in the old musicals on television. Shaft kept up, yet not too close. He wanted to see more than Caroli's back against the smoothly tailored pinstripe. But all he saw was hallway and more doors, all he heard was the grating of his shoes and those of the man in front of him as they quick-stepped up the wooden staircase. The only difference between this tenement and all the others he'd seen, he thought, was that this one smelled a little better. Not much, but nobody had pissed in the hallways recently and the owner apparently had sense enough to collect the garbage or make the tenants cart it down to the cans in front of the building. But it was still what it was: a place where trouble lived, where the poor lived, where fear lurked in large lumps behind each door.

Behind one of them, on the third floor of what Shaft had guessed to be four, was that lump of fear for which he had searched. Caroli stopped there, pulled out a set of keys on the anchor line of a slender gold rope chain.

'One thing,' Caroli said, slipping the key into an obviously new brass lock that apparently locked both inside and out with a key and only a key. 'She may not look so hot, but she's okay. She's just stoned.'

Caroli was bending over the lock as he spoke. When he turned the tumbler and finished the sentence, Shaft shot him square in the side of the head, just above the right ear. The dark, narrow hallway exploded in a flash of flame, thunder and blood. Caroli's body flew down the hall like a candy wrapper in a high wind and floated to the floor. The key chain ripped loose and dangled from the lock in the rickety door.

At that range with that gun, there was no doubt. Half of Caroli's head was sprayed onto the wall next to the door. Shaft moved before the body settled. He sprang at the door with the muscles of his left shoulder and arm bunched into a battering ram. He felt so tight he could have gone through bricks. It was more force than he needed. The old door shattered, shook and flew back against the inside wall of the room with a report that came so quickly it could have been an echo of the blast that ended Charles Caroli's life.

It was a lunge that put Shaft almost in the center of a small, dark room, crouched, black on black, the gun pointing nowhere and everywhere, weaving in his hand like a dancing cobra with five deadly fangs left to kill.

There was nothing there to kill. It was a bare room, rented as an efficiency apartment probably, with a bed, dresser, a couple of chairs and a small stove and sink set into a recess of the wall as a kitchen, a tub and a toilet jammed into a closet as a bathroom. Nothing there to kill, only the form, the small and delicate from stretched out on the bed, casting a blob of shadow against the wall in the light from a lamp on the dresser beside the bed.

Beatrice. Knocks Persons' 'baby.' Neither the shot nor the crashing of the door had disturbed her. Or if they had, her shock was spinning off into some narcotic spiral of her dreams.

Shaft never stopping moving. He jerked open the closet door and poked at the emptiness with the pistol, ripped aside the shower curtain on the tub, even bounced into a crouch and looked under the bed, put them all under the gun before he looked a second time at the girl on the bed. Time was telescoped. It all had to happen so fast. He bent over her to make sure she was breathing. It was hard to tell. She lay twisted into the folds of a sleazy light blanket. She was breathing. He picked up a corner of the gray wool rag to see what she had on. Nothing. Where were the fucking clothes? There was nothing in the closet, nothing on the chair.

He turned to the dresser. The top of it was littered with the cooking-shooting equipment of the heroin addict. Two hypos lay there, beside a candle, the bent and flame-blackened spoon, eight or nine glassine envelopes of white powder.

Shaft yanked the handkerchief out of his back pocket, poked it into a small four-corner bag over the cup of his left hand. He used the muzzle of the .38 as a tool to flip out the corners of the linen square and then poke the depression in the center of it. He also used the gun again as a prod to push all the narcotics paraphernalia off the scarred veneer of the old oak dresser into the kerchief. He was moving carefully but very quickly. The ugly, filthy hypos. They drew an involuntary shudder across his skin as they fell onto the handkerchief. People stuck those things into their skin. Somebody, probably Caroli, had been sticking them into Beatrice as she twisted across the bed.

He had thought it all out on the stairs. There was nothing to do but go as far as he could with Caroli and then reverse the direction of his action. He didn't know what was at the top of those stairs, behind the scab of a door on the sick plaster walls. He expected there would be one man, maybe two, in the room with the girl, if the girl was there at all. He expected it to be a trap of some sort for whatever reasons they chose to put him in one. There's nothing you can do with a trap except tear the motherfucker apart before it falls on you, clamps down on you, begins to squeeze the life out of you.

The lock, he thought. It was the lock in the door that told him Beatrice was probably inside, unable to get out even if she could grope through the quagmire murk of narcosis. When the lock turned under Caroli's key, Shaft decided to tear the trap apart. He killed Caroli as openers, then went plunging through the door.

But there had been no trap. At least none that he could see. He overestimated them. There had just been the three of them involved on this level – the two he had taken out at the No Name and the dead one out in the hallway. They actually had been coming up here to see Beatrice. The man really did want to deal. But the man was dead. There was no deal. There was only setting this up and getting Beatrice the hell out of there as fast as possible.

He spun around with the bag of narcotics equipment and stepped into the hallway. Caroli bled a lot for a man with only one hole in his head. There was a deepening pool of it around the body, seeping under the hallway railing. Shaft emptied the handkerchief bag over the dead man's chest. One of the needles stayed there, the second rolled off onto the floor. A glassine packet of heroin landed on Caroli's cheek and stayed there. The others spilled on the front of his shirt.

'Get you some flowers later,' he whispered, charging back into the room.

174

There were three men waiting for him beside Beatrice's bed. They had guns just like his. And their presence raised a number of questions. Where did they come from? Who the hell were they? And why didn't they kill him?

Chapter Twelve

S HAFT WAS vaguely conscious when the final kick sent him out of the back seat of the dark Pontiac and onto the pavement. He tried to put his feet down, but he couldn't find them in the red cloud of pain. The car was turning the corner and pulling away as he rolled with a groan from his knees over to his shoulder, onto his back and then his right side. It was more a croak than a groan, a gasp and exhalation of a final agony.

They had done a job on him that compared with being batted like a tennis ball against the side of a brick building ten or twelve times. His left eye was swollen shut. There was a very slight tolerance for the blood to seep through from the slash that ran through his eyebrow almost to the temple. That had been done with the flat of a pistol barrel slammed into his face, the sharp steel sight at the muzzle catching the flesh and ripping it open like a wet paper bag.

Two, possibly three, of his ribs were fractured on the left side. Black shiny shoepoints did that when he raised his arm to cover his face. Kicked him once, twice and then again as he tried to roll away. Each shallow breath was a dull knife dragging across his heart and lungs. A fourth kick that might have taken even more of the ribs had torn at the flesh above his left kidney. A fifth had got him in the base of the spine and had put him out for a few seconds in a paroxysm of shock.

The minor rips and tears were everywhere. His numb swollen

hands had been stepped on, jumped on. His lips were cracked pulpy and four or five of the teeth behind them were loose. The cartilage of his nose was as mushy as a candy bar sitting in the summer sun. His right ear was torn and swollen.

Goddamn, it hurt. It hurt so much John Shaft croaked little whimpers into the pavement, blowing blood bubbles from the froth of crimson through the swollen mouth. If he passed out, maybe the pain would go away for a little while. But if he passed out, maybe he would die because he couldn't stand to be alive with it any longer. The salt of a tear was acid in a cut on his cheek. But he could not hold it back. It hurt so bad, so bad.

There was no cohesive pattern to his thoughts. With each painful heartbeat or breath, twitch or turn, whatever was going through his mind flashed off under the assault of a throbbing red strobe. The image changed. He would hear a snatch of their voices, see them tearing at him again. When he saw the image of their fists and feet and the slashing barrel of the gun, he cringed – and the pain blinded him again. When he heard the snarl of their voices, he tried to listen, to hear if he was going to survive the beating and what they intended to do with him.

When it came to him that it was finally over and that whatever he was still existed in this pitiful puddle of bleeding flesh on the pavement, he also realized that they were gone. That was his first connected thought from the moment the beating began with the slash of a pistol barrel in the room on Thompson Street. He fainted at the simple beauty of it.

Knocks Persons watched the crumpled, ragged body sigh and shudder on the pavement in front of his brownstone castle. He saw from a window on the third floor of the building. He watched for five sad minutes. He stood silently in the tent-huge wrappings of a gold silk robe, teeth tight on the end of a lighted cigar. And having waited for Shaft to die or the enemy to reveal itself, either action being of primary importance to his generalship, he turned to a tall, powerfully built man standing in attendance beside him and said, 'Three of you go out there and get him. Take a straightback chair. Don't bend him none. Jus' lift him on that chair careful and carry him in here. Slow and careful.'

The man turned to obey.

'You hold his head while they carry him,' Knocks added. 'Don't let nothing wobble loose.'

Simple, old-fashioned first-aid. It was something Knocks thought he remembered from working in the prison infirmary. Or maybe from having been in and around so many human disasters. The man on the sidewalk was one of those now. He didn't want a fool mistake to make it any worse than it was if Shaft still lived.

He remained at the window, a silent mound of gold silk fuming cigar smoke, as his men went down the front steps in the beginning dawn. They moved cautiously but quickly. Their thoughts were the same as his, that Shaft's body was less a delivery than an invitation to mayhem. In a curious way, Persons found himself more touched and concerned by the obvious agonies of the man on the sidewalk than he had ever been for others around him who had suffered the consequences of his crimes. He did not ask himself why. It had something to do with the girl, of course. Something to do with Shaft being an extension of himself in the one area where he permitted his giant hulk to have feelings. Now he felt some of the pain as the men eased the body onto the old chair, one took the front legs, another the back and lifted him up the stairs, his head tenderly cradled in the hard black hands of a castle guard, a killer. When they were at the door, Persons turned and hurried down to take charge of what had to be done. It hurt. He knew it hurt. He, Knocks Persons, had felt the pain.

Shaft's one unswollen eye blinked open when the ice bags were being pressed against his swollen face. For one of the few times since his childhood, he woke without knowing where he was and what movements to make, whether to run, to swing, to speak or remain silent, to be alive. His reactions were clouded by pain and fury, each one struggling for dominance.

'What the . . .?' he croaked against the ice bag with grotesquely swollen lips.

'Easy,' Knocks cautioned and commanded in a grumble that bordered on a public expression of his concern. 'Easy.'

Shaft could see the blob of gold shimmering near him when the ice bag was moved away from his face and knew immediately that the hands on him were tender, not tearing.

'Where . . .?'

'My place,' Persons said. 'Rubbing some ice on you.'

Shaft tried to sit up. The pain in his side threw smothering hazes of confusion over him like a collapsing circus tent. He almost fainted again.

'Don't move,' Persons said.

'Cocksuckers,' Shaft groaned. He remembered who he hated. And almost how much.

He blinked his one green eye and lifted his left arm to look at his watch. Only the circle of the casing was still attached to his arm. The insides of it had been kicked out. His watch! It was one of the first good objects, fine objects, he had given himself. A reward for succeeding and a prize for surviving. The watch had come from Tiffany's. Someplace in his dresser, he still had the velvet-cushioned blue leather box.

'Motherfuckers,' he croaked. He was making a discovery. The angrier he became, or the more conscious he became of his anger, the less pain he felt. He let out all the stops of his fury and felt it swell through his battered flesh like the final, rising chord of a giant pipe organ. His anger roared, thundered silently. He made a foolish promise to himself. He would kick every guinea he met for the rest of his life in the wrist in the hope of smashing all their gold meshband watches.

'Knocks,' he whispered. 'Get more ice. Pack me in it.'

'Ice,' Persons commanded. The other figures in the room moved. Shaft heard cubes clinking against buckets. 'Empty the freezer downstairs. There's more in the box on the third floor. All of it.'

'What time is it?'

'Almost six.'

'Find Ben Buford. Get him here. Quick.'

'Where's he at?'

'How the fuck do I know?' That's what Shaft *thought* he said. The sound was entirely alien to his ears. He had been disconnected from himself. All the parts weren't together, working the way they should be. Somewhere between his voice and his ears, the circuits had been ripped up and torn. He was like a fighter who had to get himself back together again to answer the summons of the warning buzzer – get together or give it up. A fighter. A fuzzy notion tickled the base of his skull. His mind was trying to say something about fighters, fighting. Shit, he'd lost it.

Knocks was patient. 'What's the best way? Where do I send them?'

'His mother,' Shaft said. 'Start with mother.' He rambled around his aching head and came up with a number, an address. 'Go there. Go fast. Fast.'

He heard Knocks giving orders. But his mind was back on fighters. He saw a black boxer slumped in the corner of a Madison Square Garden ring, the bright lights nailing the figure against the stool and the ropes. It was his own body, he thought, battered and beaten. The fighter would never answer the buzzer and the bell. There was nothing left to the poor sonofabitch. The figures hovering around him, trying to exhort one last effort from him, were merciless in their insistence. His hatred focused on them. He couldn't. He wasn't an animal. He wasn't. The short, stump-shaped man in a sweatshirt was stabbing at him with a Q-Tip dipped in iodine and alum. The little bastard! He was through. Get away from him. Leave poor John Shaft to bleed. He had lost. Throw in your fucking towel and get him out of there.

In the moment of surrender, the focus of his fantasy was turned to the man with the iodine. His hands flew over the fighter's body. A man who had patched up more tattered bodies than the emergency room of Harlem Hospital. Who the fuck was it? Names of fighters came to his mind instead. Gavilan. Sugar Ray. Torres. Griffith.

'Doc Powell,' Shaft groaned. 'Doc Powell.'

The activity around him stopped momentarily.

'What he say?'

'He say somethin' 'bout "Doc Powell." That the ring man. The fight man.'

Shaft's good eye opened again.

'Get Doc Powell,' he said again, once he found the yellow mountain on his blurred horizon.

Instinct told him that Persons would understand, read his message and act. Instinct told him that the two of them were survivors; they understood that a man did what he had to do. Survivors knew what was best for themselves. They had evidence. They had survived. If Shaft needed Buford and Doc Powell, that was what he needed. That was what Persons would get for him. And it would be surprisingly easy. In Harlem, almost every black man of importance is somewhere just around the corner. Shaft let his eye close to wait.

Doc Powell got there first, even shorter, stumpier and more dwarfed than he seemed under the glare of the ring's arc lights. He bulged in a gray sweatshirt. Apparently he only wore white for formal, ten-round killings. He carried a small, black lizard-skin physician's bag. Persons' men had just hit some places where fighters hang out, places that Knocks owned. They knew where to find Powell immediately. He came without question, thinking maybe that one of the inarticulate tigers he worked for in the ring had let his fists roar for him and now needed patching – or needed someone else patched, a wife, a girlfriend, a bartender. It happened from time to time. This was a state where a fighter's fists are called weapons by the law and a man can throw away his career and the rest of his life with a left hook at a nonprofessional. Doc Powell came quickly, but he wasn't willing to stay.

'Get him to a hospital,' he said when he got a look at Shaft. 'That man been hit by a truck.'

'Do what he wants,' Knocks said.

Shaft blinked at Powell. The pain had settled into a dull clamor for his senses as long as he remained still. He was going to have to take more.

'Got to get up,' he said to the little man with the black bag. 'Get me up.'

'You need a doctor, a real doctor.' There was a plaintive note in Doc's voice, like a veterinarian being asked to do brain surgery.

'Need *you*,' Shaft said. 'Do it.'

'Get his clothes off,' Powell said. 'Gentle. Treat him like he was just a baby.'

Forty fingers came out of the periphery around Shaft, lifted, tugged and stripped him. But he wasn't sure. He was so numb.

'Ribs,' he said.

'Man, you a mess,' Powell commented.

Even the great stoic pile of Knocks Persons rumbled in appreciation of the welts, cuts, rips and bruises with a sound like a snoring volcano.

'Do it,' Shaft said. 'The ribs. Where the hell is Buford?'

The ripping of adhesive tape sounded like wood cracking. Through the haze of pain he felt the hands touching and turning him. He let his body move with the touch as much as he could. He could hear words, instructions. Powell was working like he had just a one-minute break between rounds and he had to get his man back on his feet. It was the only style he knew.

'Oh, mother!' Shaft moaned when the tape went around his chest in a two-inch hoop of hell. There were explosions of fire and sound behind his eyeballs. It was the flame and sound in which Charles Caroli's head had become a part of the tenement hallway. He kept himself conscious thinking about that moment, relishing it.

'Keep the ice on his eye,' he heard Powell order.

When his ribs were taped, he could almost breathe.

'Lemme get at that there ... This gonna hurt, boy ... Where's the tape? ... Here, you got to hold him like just so ... I get under that and wrap him up ... Damn, somebody ought to stitch that up ... That's a *bad* cut ...'

Powell's hands fluttered around the blossom of his agony like a hundred-pound butterfly. He couldn't see all of it, because most of his face was covered with icepacks. When he did get a glance through a movement of the towels, he saw a zebra-striped black body covered with lines and patches of adhesive tape and athletic bandages.

'Go get some ... gimme some more ... I need a lot of ... Where's ... You got any ...' Powell had them running.

'Get me a gun,' Shaft said.

'You don't need no gun,' Powell said. 'You ain't goin' nowheres.'

'What kind?' Knocks asked in a tone that implied somebody was waiting to go fetch it from whatever arsenal he kept.

'Forty-five,' Shaft said. 'Couple extra clips. Where the fuck is Buford?'

'Right here, looking at you,' Ben Buford said. 'You a goddamn mess.'

Shaft raised an arm to push away the icepacks. He did it automatically. But he was surprised his arm moved so easily. The tape on his chest had pulled a lot of him back together.

The right eye was open more than a slit now. He could see between the mushroom puffs of flesh that remained around it. Buford was standing at the foot of the bed. The tall, slender revolutionary looked like a teenager on his way to a stickball game in the streets. He had pulled on a blue polo shirt, a rayon jacket that gleamed electric blue under white piping, a pair of khaki slacks. How long had he been there? What had he watched of Doc Powell's ministrations and heard of his own aching response to them? Too much? Not enough? There was no sympathy in the eyes behind the glittering, gold-framed glasses. But there was no satisfaction either. At least he was not happy to see Shaft so fucked up.

A short, dark man came into the room, removing a yellow, oilskin wrapper from a bulky black object in his hand, looking to Persons for approval, then handed it to Shaft.

'How many good people you got, Ben?' Shaft asked, weighing the heavy .45 caliber automatic in his right hand. It was Army surplus, but he couldn't tell what war. The bluing had been toned down with an acid bath; everything else about the gun was dull and dark. No reflections in the night. He jacked the chamber back. A fat, stubby brass bullet climbed out of the spring in the clip and into the chamber.

'Why?' Buford asked. He seemed to have moved back a fraction of an inch in the presence of the heavy automatic and the sound of its preparation for firing.

'Put the icebag back on my eye,' Shaft ordered. He flipped the thumb safety into position on the side of the chamber, put the gun down on the bed beside his taped thigh. He let his hand lay on it. For comfort, for reassurance, for promise. But not as threat. He was not menacing Buford. The pain, the goddamned pain in his head. He stopped Doc Powell's continuing ministrations with a gesture. 'What's the strongest thing you got in that bag to stop the hurting?'

'Demerol,' Powell said.

'Gimme about four and get out of here for a couple of minutes. You done a good job.'

Shaft tried to move. His body ached, but he could sit up.

'You should stay still,' Powell said. But by this time Shaft's bare legs were dangling over the edge of the bed, touching the soft plush of a white rug. He accidentally put his right thigh down on top of the gun barrel. He flinched. Even after all the ice cubes, cold steel jarred warm flesh. 'Need some clothes.' He looked at Persons. 'Anybody around here my size?'

His own clothes were a blood-stained, ragged pile at the side of the bed. Shaft had to sit up straight under the pressure of the tape around his rib cage. He counted four or five people in the room. One of them, a duplicate of the types who always seemed to be just a little behind, a little to the right of Buford, stared at him from the lofty eminence of his revolution. Doc Powell's hands appeared in front of his face. He held four white pills and a glass of water. Shaft gulped them.

'Get some of these people out of here.'

Knocks nodded at the men. They began to leave the room. Buford just looked over his shoulder at his own companion. The man nodded and turned to go. On the way out, they stepped aside to permit the entrance of a man carrying a pair of dark slacks, a freshly laundered white shirt and Shaft's shoes. He put the clothes on the bed, the shoes on the floor.

'Thanks,' Shaft said, looking down. The shoes had been shined. He smiled as much as the cut lip permitted. Only a black man would understand the importance of the shine on those shoes. He smiled, smiled and looked up at the man whose pain ran deeper than a cut or a kick or a fracture. 'Thanks,' he said.

In a moment, the three men were alone, left with the emergency-room smells of Doc Powell's fleshmending and the ring man's words of advice: 'You just lay down if you got any brain left in yo' head.'

'Thanks,' Shaft said, willing the Demerol to dissolve in his empty stomach and take away the hurt. 'Thanks.'

He pulled on the pants without bending over, then the shirt, each movement trying a new muscle. It wasn't so bad now. He felt as fragile as an egg that had been rolled down the Grand Canyon and was still more or less intact. The shell was cracked up a little, but the insides were yet to be scrambled. Buford was waiting for an answer. Why? Shaft looked up at him.

'I can't put on my socks,' he said. He couldn't bend against the tape. He was tucking the shirt into the top of the slacks, cinching up the belt. They were a little loose and the belt's pressure added to the pain. Maybe the adhesive tape would keep them up. 'I can't bend over.'

Knocks would have done it. The mountain would have moved for Mohammed. Maybe instinct held him back, maybe the message didn't get through to him. But he didn't move and the weight of Shaft's infirmity fell on Buford.

'The man said you belonged in bed,' Buford complained, moving to the side of the bed, kneeling on the carpet and poking inside the shoes for Shaft's socks. He pulled them over the bare feet quickly but gently, using two hands like a nurse helping a surgeon into his rubber gloves. Then he slipped on the shoes and tied the laces.

'Not too tight, Ben,' Shaft said, smiling.

Buford glanced up in annoyance. 'Tie your own fucking shoes next time,' he snapped.

'I'll just go to another nigger for the shine,' Shaft dug at him. 'Cat can always find somebody to do that kind of work.'

'Shit,' Buford said.

Shaft wondered if he was getting high on the Demerol. He felt loose, cool. The hard bite of the pain seemed to have gone somewhere in the background to wait for him. Even his fury felt dulled. That drug shit, he thought. He reminded himself that he was forcing his way out of the bed for a reason.

'I want twenty, twenty-five of your people,' he said to Buford.

Ben didn't get up. He remained crouching like a giant grasshopper. One of his hands was still on Shaft's shoe. But his mind was off on the men who were passing out rifles to each other, gathering pocketsful of long, lean cartridges.

'What for?'

'I'm going to burn down Thompson Street.' He raised the empty circle of his watch casing. He unbuckled the strap, tossed the skeleton of the watch on the bed beside him. He reached down for Buford's left wrist, raised it and looked at the watch. 'In exactly thirty minutes. That's ten minutes to get the people you going to lend me, twenty minutes to get there. And I'm going to burn that motherfucker right down to the ground.'

Shaft the opportunist, Shaft the uninvolved and detached observer, Shaft the middle-man of whatever race he claimed in the depths of his heart, tried to get up off the edge of the bed to determine if he had the legs for his promise. He was

187

all mouth if he didn't have them. Persons and Buford had no response to his threat. They expected him to fall over onto his swollen face into the carpeting.

'Easy, slow,' Persons said.

'Man, you can't . . .' Buford began.

He was on his feet. His head began spinning like the propellor on a cranky, single-engine plane, a couple of jerky turns, then a few slow spins and finally a full rapid turning. He thought he might be going out and reached a hand toward Buford, still kneeling on the carpet. Buford unfolded to his feet like a portable aluminum beach umbrella. Persons moved closer, his hands also ready to catch the falling tree. Shaft struggled for a thought, a point to pin his mind on and make it stop, bring it out of the spin. Of all the images, the one that came clearest was a girl, a small black girl stretched out on a bed. Twisting spinning, turning. Please, please, please. His eyes came back into focus. The two men were standing at his sides, waiting, not touching him, but hands tentatively reaching and ready.

'Hey,' he said. 'It's easier to breathe this way. But that first shot of oxygen turns your head around.' The price of the effort was high. He felt himself begin to sweat.

'And if you ain't going to help me – ' he looked to Buford – 'I'm going to burn the motherfucker down by myself.'

His gargoyle glare taking Buford apart, pretense by pretense, promise by promise.

'I can't waste the men on some fool . . .'

Shaft broke off Buford's apology-refusal by turning to Persons.

'I ain't going to ask you but once,' he said to Buford, then turning to Persons. 'I saw Beatrice this morning.' The old man stiffened as if a spear had been plunged through the top of his shining skull. 'And as best I could tell she's all right. But you know who's got her, don't you?'

188

'I guess I do.'

'You're fucking right, you do! You know what they want for her? It's not a piece, a taste. They want *everything*. Every last stick and scrap you got. Of everything, everywhere. The whole of Harlem . . .'

'Is she . . .?'

'She's layin' in a bed sleeping. I don't know all they done to her. But it was enough to make her sleep.'

He turned back to Buford. 'Ben, there's one way to get her out of there. An easy way. Knocks gives them Harlem and they give him back the girl.'

'Nobody gives anybody Harlem,' Buford said.

'That's right, man. But you don't understand that nobody gives it to *you* either. You work for it.'

'Or take it.'

'Yeah, take it. You can take it, man. Except there's some people around who got as many guns as you got, who got as many hates as you got. When you finish counting up the dead and look around, you going to find that somebody you never even heard of before has got it. Get out of my way. I'm going to get that girl. Knocks, you got a car and a can of gasoline? Gimme some rope and newspapers.'

'Wait a minute,' Buford protested, putting out a hand. Shaft was picking up the .45 from the bed, fixing it in the belt of the trousers. He had to stoop at the knees to do it. The gun was heavier than fried bread.

'I need a jacket. Gimme your goddamn jacket if you won't give me anything else.'

He put out his hand.

'Fast, goddamnit,' he said. Buford began taking off the bright blue jacket.

'My people will go with you,' Persons said. 'How many you want?'

Silence.

'You see?' Shaft said to Buford. 'There are other people in this fucking world than just you. Other *black* people, like me, like him. When we need you, we need you bad and you ain't there because you can't waste the men. You can't waste your revolution. Well, when we *don't* need you, we don't need you at *all*. Why don't you go up on the roof and shoot some little old lady in the head while she's walking with the dog. That's your style, man.'

He was saying it all very quietly. He wanted to shout, but he couldn't take that much wind into the lungs and press them against the splintered ribs.

He expected Buford to take a swing at him. But he had the cripple's edge; he was too goddamned beat up already for anybody to hit him again. While he was talking, in fact, Buford had stripped off the jacket and handed it to him.

'No,' he said to Knocks, 'I don't want your men. I need an army, not a bunch of policy runners. An army. Because that's what's waiting down there.' Then back to Buford. 'You think you're some kind of Che Guevara, huh? Well, you ought to read about that mother. Sometime you do your homework, and not in the goddamned *Daily News*, baby. Knocks, just one man to drive the car. That's all I need.'

Knocks turned to rumble out of the room, to get the man Shaft wanted, the car, the can of gasoline, the rope.

Shaft started to walk up and down the room, slowly and carefully. He was trying out the bruised and bent portions of his body. He needed to know how much body he had left. One man, that's all he needed to commit suicide.

'Yeah,' he said, 'sometime you sit down and read about this Guevara cat.'

'You already cost me five good people,' Buford said.

'That's too stupid to argue about. When you get done with

Che, you read about some wars. There been revolutions in every country on the face of the earth. You read about them, how they fight them, how they *win* them and how they lose them.'

He was doing all right. He would be able to move. It was just that he couldn't breathe. He should have asked Doc Powell if he could take a big drink on top of the Demerol. Probably not.

'I got to get the fuck out of here,' he said, hanging on to the newel post of the bed, flexing his right leg at the knee. He had apparently been kicked in the kneecap and the thigh muscle.

'You can hardly move,' Buford scoffed at him. 'You going to get killed.'

Shaft fixed the weight of the .45 in his belt again, zipped up a couple inches of Buford's jacket to both conceal it and hold it.

'Maybe I will, Ben. But I'll know more than you will if you walk out of here and get hit by a truck going across the street. I'll know *why* and the price is going to be high. I'll know what it was for, goddamnit. I'll even know what to do tomorrow. You don't know that. You don't know anything about yesterday and you won't know anything about tomorrow. Your revolution is only for today and that ain't good enough.'

There were some tears running down Shaft's cheeks. He didn't hurt that much anymore. He rubbed them away with the sleeve of Ben's jacket.

'What's your plan?' Buford asked.

Chapter Thirteen

B EN BUFORD led fifteen men to Washington Square. They traveled in three cars and parked them in the underground garage of a luxury apartment on lower Fifth Avenue, about three blocks north of the beautiful alabaster arch at the entrance to the green. The garage attendant thought of turning them away. He would have if it had been Ben alone. Instead, he gave them tickets to his fear and the eventual claiming of the cars, watched them march out of the garage and then called the police.

'There's something funny going on . . .' he said. The announcement did not amuse the Police Department. But it did not alarm the department at first. Blacks were free to move through the city so long as they remembered to shuffle.

Three and four abreast, the revolutionary band marched down the swept, almost polished sidewalks in front of the glistening buildings that form a luxury strip of about three or four blocks below Fourteenth Street. They passed a uniformed officer lolling around the corner of Ninth Street and Fifth Avenue and they were noticed by a cruising squad car moving slowly down Fifth Avenue. The officer on the corner went to the nearest pea-green lamppost call box and the men in the car radioed their headquarters. But neither attempted to interfere with the orderly, quiet movement toward the Square. The parks of New York are for everyone, so long as they have the courage to enter them.

They were a black blotch, a smear against the towering pink

and white columns of exclusive comfort that line Fifth Avenue in these few blocks, a sooty tar patch on the fresh purity of the early morning. The black men who walk in Greenwich Village are part of the night, when their contrast does not offend the eye so sharply. This was an indignity, an outrage of blackness, these fifteen or sixteen tall, young men in dasheekis, turtlenecks, leather jackets, beads and medallions dangling around their necks. They were made the more ominous, threatening and collectively black by the discipline of their movement down Fifth Avenue toward the small, square park. They walked as a unit and a pack, not a raggle-taggle band, closely and confidently.

'All right,' Ben Buford said when they were at the northern perimeter of the park. 'Start banging on them goddamn doors. Ask the white folks what they gonna do for their black brothers today. Insult the shit out of them. Do it fast. Don't let 'em close those doors. Drag 'em out on the steps and yell at 'em.'

Two by two, they moved off to the steps of the expensive, pampered brownstones and apartment buildings that encircle the park. Buford jogged up the steps of the nearest, a red-brick and iron-trimmed residence of a corporation lawyer named Arthur J. Kravitz, who was at that moment slipping into a paisley silk robe to descend the stairs for breakfast and a perusal of *The Wall Street Journal* that the housekeeper would have put beside his coffee cup. He heard the doorbell ring, wondering what it might be at this hour. Then he heard Buford's companion pass a large geranium pot from the front steps into the entrance foyer of the house directly through one of the polished bevel-cut glass windows beside the door. Its meaning was made clear to him by a high-pitched, derisive cry that echoed through the house and brought the rest of his family to a state of consciousness, if not understanding.

'Wake up, motherfucker!' the voice rang in a clarion of terror. 'Your black brother is here for the weekend!'

In the echoes that filtered through the young, hopeful leaves on the maples and shrubs of the park, Buford could hear glass shatter and the rattle-scramble of garbage cans and lids scraping across pavement. He could see, in his mind's eye, twenty-five trembling white hands clutch nervously for the telephones to turn the switchboard of the police department into an astronomy lesson of drunken constellations. Soon, he would hear the sirens, too. He thought, looking at the black iron fence around the park, both of jail and the sonofabitch who had opened up on him with the machine gun in Detroit. He would be encircled shortly. His own people were making calls from Harlem, to every number they knew in the Village. And soon the encirclers would be encircled as well, and the mayhem would fill these streets in a great swirling, checkerboard mass of black and white.

He leaned over to the shattered window and shouted, 'Get your ass down here!'

It was a small price to pay for the whole of Harlem.

The broker of the deal wasn't so sure. Shaft thought he would collapse when they got to the third floor of the MacDougal Street building. The exertion was in forcing him to breathe hard and breathing was pushing against the bones of his ribs. Each heartbeat was a slam in the side with a two-by-four and he was drenched with sweat.

'Man, lemme take the can of gas,' urged Willie Joe Smith. His plea may have been less generous than anxious. He wondered when the moment would come that the big bandaged man leading him up the brownstone stairs would fall back upon him and grind him into the steep stairway, spilling gasoline over both of them from the two-gallon can.

'Shh,' Shaft insisted with a spit-blurred hiss.

As much as the weight of the gas and his aching body, he felt the concern of this man Persons had sent to drive him. Willie Joe Smith would go anywhere Knocks Persons sent him. He was about forty-five, square in form and concepts, and in his lexicon the places they were intruding belonged to whites, maybe even white folks, but certainly nothing approaching the psychology of Whitey. He was only there because he had been told to be there, an instruction that would have taken him to hell's front lawn of cinders for a Sunday picnic if Knocks was bringing the chicken.

He had driven the big white Oldsmobile as Shaft had directed, leading a second caravan of three cars of those wild-looking young black men down the West Side Highway and into Ninth Avenue at the Nineteenth Street exit, then up Bleecker to the point where Shaft signaled a halt, spoke with the leaders of the other groups and told Willie Joe to proceed on to MacDougal Street.

'About right here,' Shaft told him. They were midway on MacDougal between Fourth Street and Houston. Parking was tight.

'Don't put it by the fire hydrant,' Shaft said. 'They may need all they got.'

Willie Joe found a place marked RESERVED FOR DELIVERY VEHICLES.

'We delivering,' Shaft said and Willie fitted the chrome-studded Olds into the spot. The street was still empty. It was too early for anyone to be up and heading to work from these apartments, the converted brownstones that demanded the highest of rents, and too late for anyone to be getting home. If they did run into anybody, Shaft realized, he would have one hell of a time producing a spontaneous explanation of why he was there, looking as if he belonged on a shelf in Weber's Meat Market with a sign sticking in his left ear calling for ninety-eight cents a pound. But it was the least of his concerns.

He limped and wobbled as he walked to the small green-stucco foyer of a brownstone that had become an apartment house, with Willie Joe Smith coming up close behind like a child who didn't want to lose track of his mama in a strange and hostile place.

'You want me to stay here and watch?' he asked.

'Come on,' Shaft said brusquely. 'You may have to carry me the hell out of here.'

He did the plastic-card-case routine with the door lock.

'That's no trouble,' Willie Joe said.

'The only trouble comes now.'

He went up the stairs noiselessly, slowly. The gas can dragged at his hand like an anchor five inches in the mud and the metal handle worked on a bruise on his hand. Willie Joe was carrying a wad of newspapers and a coil of backyard laundry-line rope. The hallways were clean and silent, the steps covered with a tile tread that was either swept or mopped regularly. How simple it was to live cleanly, decently, he thought.

'You all right?' Willie Joe asked.

Shaft wasn't sure. He seemed to know what he was doing, but he couldn't focus his mind. There was a dream quality about doing this, being here. He felt disembodied, floating from the top of his skull out into some other place and time while his body went through these programmed motions. Where was he going again? Oh, yes, up to the roof of the building – up there to burn down Thompson Street. That's right. Keep going. One foot and then another.

He could hear a radio playing behind one of the doors on the third floor. Somebody waking up to the urgency of Jim Morrison going on

> *Come on, baby, light my fire,*
> *Baby, come and . . .*

Shaft was halfway up the steps to the fourth floor before the ridiculous coincidence struck him. The smile cracked the alum-drawn scab on his lip and he winced. The song was working in his head.

> *Shaft is gonna light your fire,*
> *Shaft is gonna light . . .*

Why? Why was he doing this? The pain asked the question. So did his continuing sense of futility that descended upon him in regard to the people involved. Hate, a job of work, a black thing, an evil thing, revenge? The questions were new to him. He was so fucking tired and lonely, puzzled by the sweeping assault of doubt. He tried to remember and the simple hurt made it difficult. He could remember the ten thousand dollars in the freezer compartment of his refrigerator. What the fuck good was it? He couldn't buy those last eight steps with it, or the roof or a breath that didn't go into him like a blunt spear.

What he remembered most, what goaded him was a barely visible, faintly discernible image of some people who thought he had been slowed to a crawl, who believed they had put him out of action while they tidied up the mess he had made in their well-organized lives and used his bleeding carcass as both the medium and the message of their purpose. He was the errand boy and what they had done to him was what they had to say. Yes, that was it, he thought. He was here because of that, within the hour of their relaxation and confidence that he had been dealt with for more than enough hours. He was still John Shaft. That was enough. He had earned the right to believe it.

'Can you climb that?' Willie Joe whispered.

Shaft reached up for a rung of the narrow steel ladder rising out of the fourth floor toward the TV antenna jungle of tarpaper rooftops.

'If I can't,' he said, 'I'm going to fly. Come right up behind me. If I start to slip, push my ass up through that hole.'

Twelve rungs, one at a time, each one a little slower, sometimes an arm around the ladder rather than a hand on the rungs, but making it. He pushed the top off the access porthole in the roof with his head. He simply couldn't lift his arm with the gas can. He crawled out onto the tarpaper and stayed there on his hands and knees, his body begging for repayment of the spent strength. Willie Joe bent over and touched his shoulder.

'How can I help you?'

'Lemme breathe a minute,' Shaft gasped. He sucked shallow gulps of air, fighting himself not to take too much, balancing the desperate need against the crippling pain. He was barely able to raise his head and look around. Rooftops were all alike, Harlem or the Village, Beekman Place or Hell's Kitchen. Nobody could see it, so nobody gave a damn what it was like, except where people used them for summer sun and sootbaths. These were spring roofs, collections of tar cans as mementoes of winter's emergency pluggings.

'Look for boards,' he told Willie. 'Planks, long as you can find. Over there.' He pointed his head toward the next roof where some construction seemed to be underway on the housing for an elevator control system or an air-conditioning plant.

'What you want boards for?' Willie Joe asked.

'I can't jump these buildings. We got to walk across. Hurry.'

Willie Joe started moving, a big brown chipmunk scurrying across the rooftops gathering peanuts, here, there, then back again. There were boards all over the rooftops. It was a place to store them for the building custodians whose basements were already cluttered with trashpiles. Shaft started to get to his feet and the .45 fell out of his waistband onto the roof with a heavy thud.

'Not yet, baby,' he said, hoping he wasn't directly above the bedroom of a burglary-nervous old maid. He didn't move for a moment and waved Willie Joe to a silent pause in his scavenging. He stooped to pick up the gun, got the gas can and tiptoed to the rear edge of the roof. The chasm between this MacDougal Street building and the one facing Thompson was only eight feet. He didn't think the opposite number across the small alley was the one he wanted, but he'd have to look down into the street to tell. By then, Buford's men would be in front of the place. They had the number.

Willie Joe had a stack of ten- and twelve-foot boards ready for the bridge. Together, Shaft helping as much as he could, they eased them out into the air, one by one, touching the opposite parapet and then setting them into place.

'These things hold us?' Willie Joe asked.

'What else is there?' Shaft grumbled impatiently. He regretted it. What right did he have to put down this man who was helping him? Willie Joe had run his share of tenement rooftops. He was as calm about leaning over the parapet to build their bridge as a window washer dangling on the edge of eternity against the assurance of heavy leather safety straps. There were no straps for Willie Joe except his toes digging into the center of balance in his shoes.

Shaft thought he heard noises in the distance, rumble noises of a mob. So soon? Where were the sirens? Or was it the rumble of his own anxiety? It told him to hurry. He looked out at the boards across the space between the buildings and felt his mouth turn dry.

'Listen,' he said to Willie Joe. 'I can't walk that. I'm going across on my hands and knees. If I fall, just get the fuck out of here. There ain't nothing left to do after that.'

Willie Joe nodded. Shaft guessed the man had enough to do with his rope and the papers. The way his head was spinning, the way the twinges kept coming at him from new directions with each movement, he couldn't risk eight feet without a wobble or lurch. He got up on the parapet on his hands and knees, careful not to shake the boards loose at either end. The gas. He had to take the gas can. He put it out on the planks in front of him, bent over and gripped the handle in his teeth. It forced his head straight down. One thing, he couldn't look over the edges of the plank. He didn't need to. He knew what was down there.

A few inches at a time, as far as he could move one knee and then the other. One thing about big pain, he thought: it gets rid of all the little pains. It also made him want to just stretch out face down on the boards and forget about it all, high above an alley, let it all go floating by. His ears began to ring with a screaming clangor of pounding blood. If it got any stronger, his head would explode. Inch by inch, keep moving. It got louder. He discovered that it wasn't his head; it was every siren in the city wailing toward Washington Square. There must be one hell of a brawl beginning there. The drop of pleasure falling on a sea of pain stirred laughter in Shaft's depths. He couldn't let it out. He had to grind his teeth on the gas-can handle. He had to hurry. The time was now.

Anderozzi got the phone on the second ring.

'Yes.'

'It's happening in Washington Square,' the Commissioner said.

'I wondered what all the sirens were about.'

'The Tactical Force responded, but it's the goddamndest riot they've ever seen.'

'Why?'

'There's nobody to fight except white people. There's about fifteen or twenty black bastards up in the trees throwing pop bottles and insults at a lynch mob of whites from the apartment houses around the Square.'

'What are they doing?'

'They're protecting those bastards in the trees by hitting a lot of decent citizens over the head.'

'That's smart.'

'Hang on.'

Anderozzi waited while the Commissioner got his emergency phone. He used the pause to work his arms into the sleeves of his jacket, hanging on the back of the chair. He was going to be traveling. Was Shaft in a tree? He hoped so. It sounded like Shaft.

'It's all changed,' the Commissioner rattled at him.

'How?'

'Blacks from all over the Village pouring into the Square behind the whites, trapping them between the police. It's a hell of a brawl now.'

'Who's in the trees?'

'We'll wish we were when the Mayor hears about it. I'm going down there. I'll pick you up on the way.'

Shaft peered over the edge of the far parapet into Thompson Street. They were standing to either side of a building three doors down. That was the one. He moved toward it, over the cindered asphalt of the roofing, cautiously lifting a leg over the barriers he would have leaped as a youth, hurrying as much as he could. When he reached the building he wanted, Shaft took the newspapers from Willie Joe. He crumpled the sheets into a huge ball around three twisted paper logs and tied it all together with the rope. He lowered it quickly over the edge until it dangled like a newsprint moon outside a shade-covered window on the third floor. There was a brick lying on the asphalt beside the ledge. Shaft used it as a counterweight to secure the end of the rope, then began to work with the gasoline.

'Willie Joe,' he said, dripping gas onto the taut line, watching it run down and soak into the paper as quickly as he poured it. 'I'm going down into the building.' The fumes of the gasoline worked through the mushy cartilage of his nose. He liked the smell.

'I'll go with you, man,' Willie Joe said. 'You ain't in no shape to go alone.'

'Shut up and listen. You going to hear some shooting. As soon as you do, light a match to this rope. You got a match?'

Willie Joe fumbled in his pockets. He came up with matches.

'Just put a match to it and get the hell out of here as fast as you can go. Back the same way. Anybody bothers you, tell'em you made a delivery. You got it straight, man?'

'I got it.'

'See you later, Willie Joe.'

He kicked the lid off the rooftop hatch simply because it was easier than bending over. He peered down. Same sort of ladder. But it would be easier going down. The gas can was more than half empty. A gallon's weight made a lot of difference. It would make a hell of a torch outside the window, too. He glanced at Willie Joe, standing next to the rope as he was letting himself down the hatch, feeling for the rungs with his feet. He wanted to wink at the man. His eyes were so swollen he couldn't.

Shaft was at the bottom of the ladder in a minute or so. Even there, in the dark hallway, he could hear the sirens raging outside. Ben Buford, just hang in there, he thought. Just hang in there long enough to let ten black men loiter in front of a building on Thompson Street because there ain't nobody, nowhere, who wasn't busy right now. Nobody who could ask them questions, make them move along.

At the stairwell, Shaft peered down the narrow slot of the zigzag descent. He could see all the way to the first floor. He tipped the gas can and let the rest of it slosh into the emptiness, dripping and splashing on each set of stairs as it fell, filling the building with the raw, unmistakable fumes of disaster. An hour ago, they kicked him down those stairs like a bag of empty beer cans. He threw the can down the crevass and listened to it rattle and echo emptily to the bottom. He got the .45 out of his belt, found an extra clip in the pocket of the jacket.

'Fire!' he bellowed as loudly as short breath would permit. 'The goddamn building is on fire! Fire!'

He pointed the black cannon to the roof and squeezed. The explosion shook a shower of dust and plaster down around him.

'Fire!' Bang! Bang! Bang! Three more into the roof. 'Fire! We're trapped!' Bang! Bang! Bang! That was seven. Still one in the chamber. He flicked the catch on the empty cartridge clip and let it fall to the floor as he slammed the fresh one into the handle.

Bang! Bang! Bang! It felt good. It was the Fourth of July, Hallowe'en and the Alamo all at once. He found breath in the exhilaration, ignored the pain and let out a hideous, grating scream. 'I'm burning to death! Fire!' Bang! Bang! Bang! Six from eight cartridges left two in the clip, one in the chamber. He dug for the second spare clip as he let the three rip into the roof.

He had killed Charles Caroli in the hallway of this building and there wasn't a goddamn peep out of anybody. Now the rat's nest was coming alive. Shouts, screams and shrieks echoed from the apartments along the hallways. Doors flew open.

'Gas!' a man's voice cried out. 'The building's full of gas.'

'Fire!' Shaft shouted. 'Niggers! The niggers are coming!'

A woman screamed. More doors slammed open. He could hear people running, stumbling, falling. He screamed again. It was beautiful. He was imitating the victim in a Grade B horror movie. He changed clips in the gun, jacked a bullet into the chamber. That was all he had. He started for the dark stairs, listening to the churning mass of confusion he had caused, listening for the voices of the ones he wanted.

Slowly, easily, Shaft leaned against the wall and went down the stairs sideways, left foot down first. A door flew open above him and he spun to face a woman in a nightgown and a man in his shorts. She screamed. The man looked stunned.

'Right this way. Police Department. Keep calm. Right this way.' They plunged toward the bedlam. They *were* the bedlam.

He waved them on with the .45. They fell past him in blind panic, hysteria. When they were two flights below him, part of a fighting, struggling mass to get out of the building, he fired two more shots into the air. He could pick the woman's scream out of eight or ten that responded. She was a great screamer. This was the hallway. The last of Charles Caroli had been wiped from the wall. The door was open, its new brass lock glittering innocently. He looked in, knowing it would be empty. The bed was bare. There was nothing. Cigarette smoke curled up from an ashtray on the dresser. A great red ball of flame hung outside the windows. The heat of an inferno curled the shade and pushed against his face. Shaft turned to move down the next flight. It was roaring madness below him. He had never heard so many obscenities, even in the pain of war. What would happen in a real fire?

He kept going against the wall, slowly, carefully, the gun high, ready. In a second now ... in a second now ... He heard the feet coming up the stairs as fast as feet can go. Then the face appeared. Shaft remembered it well. He always would. The face was shocked, incredulous, so disbelieving that it ran right up to the muzzle of the .45 before Shaft squeezed the trigger and blew it off.

He stepped over the body and kept moving. On the second floor landing, he found Beatrice. She was out and there was nothing to cover her. A beige doll tossed into the corner. He wasn't even sure she was alive. The one up there, the one without a face, had probably been carrying her down behind the others. Where were they?

Shaft stooped and put his left arm under the girl's right arm and shoulders. Her head fell back loosely, her mouth open. His right arm went under her knees, the gun still out front. He expected to die trying to lift her. She was remarkably light. He held her in his arms for a minute and turned to the last set of steps. He staggered on the twinge of a failing tendon in his left knee, then straightened. This he had to do, this he had to make. The whole fucking building would go up any second in the raw stink of gasoline.

Shaft heard a shot from the streets, then two quick ones in response. He went down the stairs like a zombie carrying the bride of Frankenstein. He was saying something, sobbing and blinking his eyes to keep them clear. He couldn't hear himself above the shouting from the street as he approached the doorway. But the muffled chant was part of the chorus of frenzy.

'Kill the cocksuckers. Kill them. Kill them. Kill them.'

He couldn't stop at the doorway. One lead leg after the other, he staggered out onto the top step of the building. There was a small mob in the street. He could make out black faces, dancing up and down, white people in their underwear, fists flying. There was a body in the street. No, two. He looked up Thompson and saw a car moving through the mass, pushing people aside with its fenders and bumpers. A fat man in a bathrobe didn't get out of the way in time. The car went over his leg and he screamed, then rolled into the mass around him.

'Bless your black ass, Willie Joe,' Shaft said, or maybe thought. He was never quite sure because at the moment of the words, he fainted.

Chapter Fourteen

'WHERE ARE you going?'
   Silence.
'John?'
'Hunh?'
'I asked where you were going.'
'Oh.'
Shaft sat in the middle of the living-room floor, legs folded under each other in an Indian squat.
   'I dunno,' he said. 'Away.'
   He studied the tri-level plastic device on the floor carefully. The kid had beaten him four games out of five in three-dimensional tic-tac-toe and he had actually been trying. It was embarrassing. Helen Green gazed affectionately at the hulk of him against the beige carpet with her son, the two of them concentrating fiercely. Her son's hand moved quickly to the game.
   'I win!' he shrieked.
   'Damn!' Shaft said.
   'I win, I win, I win, I win! You're lousy.'
   The little bastard didn't have to be so cocky about it.
   'I never saw this game before tonight,' Shaft defended himself. 'You had practice.'
   'That's enough,' Helen said. 'Pick that up and take it to your room.'
   'I want to beat him again,' the boy protested.

'Maybe he doesn't want to be beat again,' she said. Shaft was twice stung.

'Mind your mama,' he said. 'I'll get you next time.'

'No you won't, no you won't, no you won't,' the boy chanted. 'I win, I win, I win.'

He grabbed up the plastic shelves of the game and scooted out of the living room, chanting all the way. Shaft reached out and swatted him on the tail as he went past. Then he continued to stare at the rug where the game had been played and lost. Next time. He'd get it next time because his mind would work on it and he'd beat the kid. Then he'd have to start throwing the games so he wouldn't feel bad.

'How long will you be gone?'

'Hunh?'

'You aren't hearing me,' she said.

'Yeah. Well,' he sighed, getting up off the floor, still favoring the right leg a little where the ligament had been torn and was still mending, under heavy strapping. 'Yeah.'

Shaft walked over to the heavy crystal decanters that Marvin Green found in those good little Second Avenue antique shops like Eris on his lunch hour, haggling with some nice young guy with a funny mustache. What was his name? Harris. Harris something.

'What's the name of that antique dealer where Marvin gets these things?'

'Harris Diamant,' she said. 'A shop called Eris.'

'I know that. Just couldn't remember the man's name. Nice man.'

'Yes,' she said, watching the glass in Shaft's hand glow amber as he poured almost two inches of Scotch into it. 'How did it go today?'

He was sipping the Scotch straight, without ice. He wasn't

hearing anything she said. He took a long pull at the whisky and looked at the glass, frowned at it.

'How long did Marvin say he would be?' he asked, as if her husband was lurking somewhere in the bottom of the liquid in the tumbler.

'An hour or so. He said a client was being audited and had panicked. He had to get it straight for the Internal Revenue people.'

'Yeah. Well.' He drank some more.

'John,' she insisted. 'Listen to me a minute.' He turned his face to her, if not his attention. There were new scars, still red and angry scars, as companions for the saddle stitching of the bicycle chain. 'What went on with the grand jury today?'

He snorted.

'Not much,' he said. 'They decided I wasn't a murderer. They come out with something they call a no bill. Prosecutor chewed on me hard.' He paused to think of the district attorney's anger. 'But what the hell, I been chewed on before, will be again. Just reminded me what the rules are about being a detective. Said I violated about a hundred seventy-seven laws.'

'What laws?'

'Well, there's a lot of gun laws, for one thing. Then there's some shooting laws. And then there's some killing laws. And some setting-fires laws. All kinds of laws. It figured out to be about hundred seventy-seven I broke. Technically.'

'Are you in trouble?'

'No.' He drank deeply again, reached back for the decanter. 'I had some help.'

'Who?'

'Police Commissioner, for one.'

He thought about the short, bald and direct little man who had the balls to tell a grand jury that the four men who died on Thompson Street were the worst, the very worst of men, police records down to the floor, killers every one of them. Kidnappers, drug peddlers. Gangsters in the act of holding a nineteen-year-old girl for extortion, feeding her heroin. They happened to die while a licensed agent was performing a service for a client. They were very violent men. Violence surrounded them. They attracted it and lived by it. This time, they did not survive it. He went on to say that they had previously killed the five Negroes in the Amsterdam Avenue shooting. But he did not say that the dying may have prevented the deaths of hundreds. Nor did he say anything at all to Shaft. He glared at him as he entered the grand-jury room and glared at him as he left. Only later did Shaft learn what he had done in the rarest of appearances by a Commissioner before a grand jury – in payment for the tanks that would not roll the streets.

'Him and some others,' Shaft said. 'Listen, there's no point in my hanging around. I think I'll get down to my pad and get some things done.'

'But Marvin wants to see you.'

'Yeah. Well.' He sipped the Scotch. 'I got to get out of here before I drink all this whisky. Listen, that brown envelope there ... uh ... it's got like fifteen thousand dollars cash in it – '

'*What?*'

'– so I wouldn't let the kids play with it. It's ... uh ... a fee. But you tell Marvin that nobody's going to report it being paid to me and he's to do what he thinks best about the taxes and things and putting it in the bank. I mean, he wants to just salt it away somewhere, that's all right. Tell him the fee was ... Never mind. I'll tell him sometime.'

Shaft had nearly five thousand more in his pocket. He put the glass down on the *Ladies' Home Journal* to protect the veneer of the coffee table.

'Listen, I'll be in touch,' he said, limping toward the closet, finding his belted, brown raincoat and plunging arms into it impatiently. She followed him toward the door, reaching up to fix the collar.

'Why don't you wait and tell him?' she persisted.

'That's all right,' he said. 'I'll give him a call.'

He had to get the hell out of there. His nerves were as ragged as the old gray suit he pushed down the incinerator that morning. If anybody could look at nerves, they'd probably see old gray suit threads, torn at the shoulder, coffee- and water-stained, rumpled and weary and worn. He couldn't stand women fussing with his clothes. Her hand at his collar made him twitch.

'Yeah,' he said, 'I'll give him a call when I get back. Week or so. 'Bye.'

He leaned over to let her kiss him on the cheek. She held the lapel of his raincoat for a moment, then moved her hand to his arm.

'John,' she said, 'please take care of yourself.'

'Yeah,' he said automatically, not caring, feeling so sad about not caring and wondering why he did not feel and why he was sad. 'Well . . .'

He turned and limped down the hallway, found the elevator mercifully waiting at the floor when he pushed the button. He looked back. Helen Green was standing at the door. He waved a little flip of fingers and got in.

Some others had spoken for him. Knocks Persons for another. He had put the whole of Harlem rackets on the line for the grand jury. That and the story of Beatrice and how she was in a place called Gracie Square Hospital, getting off the horse, getting her head turned around. Knocks didn't tell them about Ben Buford and that this was the price he paid to get her there. He just told them enough about what he did for a living and what Shaft did for him. Enough. And some others spoke.

Shaft shrugged deeper into the raincoat and felt cold, even in the spring afternoon that was making promises about summer.

Cold, lifeless, drained. The motherfuckers had taken it out of him. He had to get it back.

'Hey, John!' the voice called from the Plymouth sedan.

Oh, shit! Couldn't he go *anywhere*, do *anything* without this?

'Want a ride downtown?' Anderozzi asked from the front-seat window of the unmarked police car.

Shaft walked up to the side of the vehicle.

'No,' he said. 'I'm going to get a cab.'

'Give you a ride to a cab stand.'

'No,' said Shaft.

'You all right?'

'Getting there.'

'It was a rough one.'

Shaft bent over with a twinge in his chest to see who was driving. Nobody he knew.

'It was rough,' he agreed.

'Okay, John,' Anderozzi said. 'Here.' The hawk-faced lieutenant handed a brown paper bag out the window of the car. Shaft took it. The package was heavy. He opened it and looked inside. It was the .38 from the hook under the No Name bar, the gun that had taken out Charles Caroli.

'Put that back where it belongs,' he said.

'Will there be a kick later?'

'No. No kicks later. It's all taken care of. You sure you don't want a ride?'

'No,' Shaft said. 'One thing.'

'Yes?'

'When the fuck can I start moving around without being followed?'

'Right now,' Anderozzi said with a wave. The car moved away from the curb. 'See you.'

'Not if I see you first,' he said to the departing license plate.

He turned to hunt a cab. Done, done, done. It was over. Knocks was paying the dues, Buford was collecting them. The silly sonofabitch would think he cleaned up Harlem after a while. Maybe he had. There were some cars. None of them cabs. Buford wouldn't know what to do with a clean Harlem now that he had it. Making speeches to retired pushers? Shit.

There was a cab with its dome light on. Shaft waved. It wasn't going to stop. He stepped off the curb and walked directly into the path of the car and stood facing it with his hands on his hips. He watched the dome light switch to the off-duty signal. But he stood there and the driver climbed on the brake and stopped, a goggle-eyed driver poking his head out the window.

'Off duty,' he said.

'Police business,' Shaft responded, reaching for his wallet and his identity card.

'Oh,' the driver said. 'Okay.' He reached behind him and unlocked the door. Shaft got in, putting the wallet back without showing the driver anything. To hell with him.

'Where to, mister?'

'Kennedy.'

'The airport?'

'Yes.'

'Christ,' the driver protested, setting the car in motion.

Shaft folded his arms across his chest and wriggled back into the corner of the cab. He would go to sleep. When he got to the airport he would buy a ticket. The first name that came to his head. San Francisco, Paris, Tokyo. The first name that came out. He'd go there. He'd get out of this city, out of these people, out of his own skin someplace. Stockholm, he thought. Rio de Janeiro. He played with names and continents. Nobody would know him, nobody would want him. He would lose himself. He would let the smell of death wash away with each mile, each strange place, each new person he encountered. He wouldn't even give them his right name. They wouldn't know who he was or what he was. And that would make them even.

Bloomsbury Film Classics Series

Title	Author	Price	ISBN	Qty
The Blackboard Jungle	Evan Hunter	£6.99	0 7475 3184 6	.....
Bullitt	Robert L. Pike	£5.99	0 7475 3185 4	.....
Diva	Delacorta	£4.99	0 7475 3182 X	.....
Psycho	Robert Bloch	£5.99	0 7475 3181 1	.....
The Lady Vanishes	Ethel Lina White	£5.99	0 7475 3188 9	.....
Once Upon a Time In America	Harry Grey	£7.99	0 7475 3186 2	.....
Scarface	Armitage Trail	£5.99	0 7475 3183 8	.....
Vertigo	Boileau & Narcejac	£5.99	0 7475 3187 0	.....
Cape Fear	John D. MacDonald	£5.99	0 7475 3776 3	.....
Serpico	Peter Maas	£6.99	0 7475 3779 8	.....
Shaft	Ernest Tidyman	£6.99	0 7475 3777 1	.....
The Postman Always Rings Twice	James M. Cain	£4.99	0 7475 3778 X	.....
Deliverance	James Dickey	£6.99	0 7475 4088 8	.....
The Stepford Wives	Ira Levin	£5.99	0 7475 3802 6	.....
All the President's Men	Carl Bernstein and Bob Woodward	£8.99	0 7475 4809 6	.....
The Hustler	Walter Tevis	£6.99	0 7475 3972 3	.....
The Boys from Brazil	Ira Levin	£6.99	0 7475 4238 4	.....
Marathon Man	William Goldman	£6.99	0 7475 3973 1	.....
The Man Who Fell to Earth	Walter Tevis	£6.99	0 7475 4264 3	.....
The French Connection	Robin Moore	£6.99	0 7475 4821 8	.....
A Kiss Before Dying	Ira Levin	£6.99	0 7475 4816 1	.....

Name ....

Address ....

....

.... Postcode ....

I enclose a cheque for £ .... (made payable to Bookpost Plc)

Please debit my Mastercard/ Visa/ Amex (delete as applicable) by £ ....

Credit Card Number ....

Please complete the order form and return to:

Bookpost Plc, PO Box 29
Douglas, Isle of Man, 1M99 1BQ
Tel: 01624 836000   Fax: 01624 837033
Email: bookshop@enterprise.net

Please allow 28 days for delivery

For a free catalogue of all Bloomsbury titles, please contact:
The Publicity Department, Bloomsbury Publishing Plc, 38 Soho Square,
London W1V 5DF